HAREY

By

ARLENE WEBB

cs

Decadent Publishing Company
www.decadentpublishing.com

This book is a work of fiction. Names, characters, places, and incidents are the products of the author's imagination or used fictitiously. Any resemblance to actual events, locales or persons, living or dead, is entirely coincidental.

Harey
Copyright 2015 by Arlene Webb
ISBN: 978-1-61333-825-4
Cover art by Tibbs Designs

Published by Decadent Publishing Company
www.decadentpublishing.com

Printed in the United States of America

~DEDICATION~

Many thanks to the editors at DP, and to my critique partners, especially Barbara Elsborg who has been there for me every step of the way.

Chapter One

In the year of our Lord, AD 612

$\mathcal{B}$lood trickled down his face and splattered off his chin. Bright red droplets marked leaf and grass, the sharp aroma increasing the lust of the beasts behind him. The baying of the lead hound vibrated closer and closer. Gwas's left foot came down hard and then the right. He tucked his head low to avoid another branch cracking open his forehead as adrenalin surged and panic fueled his heartbeat.

He twisted to the left, toward the light, and out of the dense thicket. They would have to risk the footpath. The little hare frantically hopped on his heels, unable to reach top speed while dodging roots, foliage, and blasted rocks. Gwas yearned to scoop up his friend, curl into a ball, and fight his shivers under a clump of brush but giving into terror assured that they would die in a very painful way. The race to survive seemed more than excruciating enough on its own.

His lungs burned like he had swallowed a sharp sword. The hurt brought tears to his eyes as he fought against his need to breathe. Bitty's lean brown body could readily absorb the force between air and ground produced by running at extreme speed, but Gwas was only a clumsy human. What he had in common with his four-footed friend was, so far, a short existence.

His heart ached. He had watched Bitty's birth but three full moons ago. The littlest in a litter of five, she would not be ready to play with a buck for at least three more months. She would never get a chance to become a mum if her worthless protector could not find an escape.

He burst free from the soft pine needles, and swallowed his yelp as his bare toes smacked into the dirt and pebbles of the steep pathway. No time to howl; relentless gray dogs capable of bringing down a wolf had their scent. His knees pumped hard, and he wondered if the friction would soon cause what little flesh he had on his bones to disintegrate, leaving the hunters a skeleton for a trophy.

Bitty sprung ahead of him—uphill and to the south—and Gwas gulped his despair. He did not dare pause. Focused on her long, black ears, leader became follower.

"Bit, no. Other way." The dumb hare not only failed to cooperate, the dash of speed he needed to keep pace left Gwas pounding the ground so fast his heart screamed to explode out of his chest.

With a half mile of intense climbing, hounds right behind them, the only way to postpone the inevitable was to climb into the highest and thickest pine he could push his aching limbs up into. If only Bit would slow and let Gwas catch her. A fat tree, lowest branch within his reach, loomed to his left, but he worried he would cost them what little lead they had managed if he stopped, caught some air, and the bloody hare hesitated to obey his whistle.

Another sharp jab in his side threatened to knock

him to his knees and his vision blurred. He jerked out of his stumble, blinked blood and tears from his eyes, and continued after his friend who had to be the most ignorant creature in existence. He would rather they had their throats ripped out by vicious, swift hounds than risk the dark presence that frequented the clearing. That gurgling splash Bitty ran toward could only be the high waterfall, a spot where *she* frequently bent her knees in quiet devotion.

A sharp rock sliced into his foot, and Gwas went down. His knee hit hard, and he tumbled off the edge of the path. The fists of the rough terrain beat into his scrawny body until his back smacked firm dirt and he lay still. It did not take long before his nightmare became actuality. He shuddered as he smelled the scent of an unwashed woman looming over him.

"Oh, you poor darlin' lad." The low soprano of a familiar voice cooed in harmony with the cascading water.

Gwas forced his eyes open. Full breasts tumbled from the loosened brown robe as the lady leaned over him. The heat on her beautiful face deepened, and Gwas prayed he would soon be dead. He could only hope that somehow Bitty survived. *Please, please, please don't turn me into a rat. Kill me clean.*

Monacella, rebel daughter to some fearsome king named Addwyn, glared down at him and Gwas swallowed hard. He had bitten his tongue. Blood coated his throat, his limbs frozen as nausea filled his shriveled belly.

"On your feet, little one." Her whisper, notes so sensual they made his head spin, resonated in the sun-bathed clearing. "Simple bastard, how dare you? Hunters, certain to be male, approach this sacred grove. You shall pay dearly for your blasphemy."

Gwas did not move, not even a blink to clear his

vision. He fought his instinct to sob and grovel. He knew his lack of fear would stimulate her rage even further. His back bore testimony to the many times he had angered her. Perhaps she would become so intent on making him scream, she would not look for the hare running fast enough to almost reach the open sea by now. Not that the little hare could swim, but perhaps she would tunnel into the soft sand and hide until kinder, less vicious predators stalked the night.

The lady turned. Horror seized Gwas and he lifted his head. A toss of his throbbing head and fluid, blood and tears splattered to clear his sights. A rush of movement, a stunning leap toward them, and his horror became despair. His brave friend had not only remained, she tried to help him. Bitty charged into the lady.

Gwas scrambled to his feet. Monacella looked down at the hare battering her robe with her forepaw. A short laugh burst from the woman. She pressed her lips tight as four wolfhounds crashed through the thicket and leaped down the incline.

Gwas dove for his friend—the lady's slender foot struck his cracked forehead. Splinters of pain jabbed from ear to ear, and he found himself again sprawled on his back. He jerked up his head. Blood splashed off his face, and he fought back his scream. Bitty scampered under the lady's robe, and the woman's snort sent shivers along his spine.

"Stand and face your gender, bane of mine, before I step on you and flatten that foul pisser of yours."

The dogs stopped twenty feet back, barking their lust, but the beasts were not dimwitted. They feared the lady as much as Gwas did. Snot and spittle flew from muzzles, sharp teeth bared. He yearned to roll from the woman's feet into the jaws of the dogs, strangle at least one of them before they spilled his lifeblood, but he scuttled backward and backward. *Bitty!* He forced himself to stop and pushed himself onto his shaking legs.

The lady stood tall, too far away from him. She ran her fingers under one full breast, cupping herself before she tightened the folds of her long robe around her neck. He frantically dropped his gaze. If only he were brave like an eagle. He would fly, swoop down, and peck her eyes out. His friend peeked at him from beneath the hem of the dirty robe and anguish filled him.

Bitty was as dead as he was. The hare would fatten the belly of the lead hound. Then he would be forced to clean every spec of fur and bone defiling the lady's sacred clearing. He would work until she had no further use for him, and it would finally end. He would not see another sunrise after his eyeballs simmered over the fire he would have built, along with his ears, toes and fingers, leaving what was left of him to slowly bleed out beneath the whip.

No! No! No! He had to try harder. Bit would run for freedom, while Gwas took on the hounds, and then he would at least die fast. The lady would go down if he bashed her in the stomach. Fists raised, Gwas charged like a crazed mother bear.

The air swooshed toward him, and Gwas did not cry out as metal and wood slammed into his calf, but he did fall flat. Hot pain shot through his left leg. Along the pathway, the rumble of horse hooves resonated. The garish sunlight around him became tainted, filled with spots of black as he shoved himself to his feet and braced for the next arrow to drive into his heart. The lady smirked at him as he stood bleeding before her. He shivered. Best not to die looking at a woman. He lowered his sight to her feet where the hare quivered. *Fare thee well, my friend. Sorry I could not save you.*

"Silent! Down!" The rough bark of a male voice stung the air. A grey horse with a black nose cantered into the clearing. A man with the deepest blue eyes glared at the dogs—and stole the air from Gwas's lungs. *He is scary and beautiful and so big.* The hounds went quiet, snarling with frustration as they fell to their bellies.

"Argo, you arse. Stay your bow. You hit a young lad." The blue-eyed man glared at the pair of men riding up beside him. The even larger man with a face full of brown and gray hair, on what had to be the biggest black beast in all the world, spurred his horse in front of the others. He clutched his weapon, a spear the size of Gwas.

"Lord, I saw him advance on the woman," the archer snapped at the bearded giant. "I thought him a man from the distance."

Blue eyes hot with anger, the younger man snarled. "Have you lost your vision? He barely reaches her chin."

As he took notice of the lady, the larger man's eyes widened. "Oh lord, fuck me now. Argo, Gareth, I claim the pretty lass." The man shifted his gaze, glancing at Gwas, and he fought the urge to splatter piss down his leg. "You deem the stripling a threat, Argo, loose the dogs on him. Your sight and aim does leave much to be desired."

The heavy-set archer lowered his bow. He scowled at Gwas then spun his attention to the lady.

Blue eyes still stared at Gwas. Plaited into thick braids, his tousled blond hair brushed broad shoulders, his kind face long and lean. Younger than the other two, his facial hair had been removed. Gwas swallowed hard. He had never seen men up close before. Not in his wildest nightmares had he imagined them to be so frightening, yet the one of them without spear or bow had eyes prettier than the sparkling of the summer sky.

The dominant male swung his thick leg around to dismount. He reeked of a musky arid scent. A strange longing, a desire to feel a heavy arm encircle his shoulders, filled Gwas. He wished the younger man would lay hands upon him, ease the pain from the metal arrowhead lodged in his leg, crafted to kill a hare with minimal damage to its flesh—and then break Gwas's miserable neck before the vindictive lady placed a spell on them all.

The leader tossed his reins to the archer and approached. He had to be either insane or bewitched, and Gwas inched toward the blue-eyed man.

One sharp glare from the lead male and Gwas froze. A wolf smile filled his bearded face and the man gawked at the lady. His sight fell from her stern visage, lingered on her breasts, dropped south to her toes, and rose again. He chuckled as he noted the cowering Bitty pressed against her ankle.

The leader dipped his head. "That hare bothering your lovely foot is mine. As are you, I pray. To show my devotion, upon your wish I shall command Argo to finish the job. The aggressive lad offended you? You would prefer him gutted?"

The lady raised her gaze and batted her eyes. "Nay. It...he frightens me, but his salvation has been my cross to bear. The byproduct of a vile rape fifteen years past, he killed his mother, my unfortunate maid upon his arrival. His wet nurse passed on a year later, worn out from his care. An insolent devil, he pretends to weed the garden. He is supposed to keep the varmints out, but instead befriends them." Her smile demure, she tossed her long hair back. "Who are you?"

"Brochfael Ysgythrog, prince and lord of Powys. I own these lands, from mountains to the sea. And, my beautiful trespasser, who may you be?"

"An unhappy daughter by the name of Monacella. My father, King Cyfwlch Addwyn, wished me to marry a nobleman. At the age of eight, I took a vow of celibacy. Until this moment, I have not seen the face of a man since I fled my father's dominions."

Liar! I hate her. And Gwas hated himself for being a coward. He should warn these mighty men to run, before it was too late for them as well.

A low grunt of surprise fell from Brochfael's lips. "You are a virgin? A recluse on my land?"

The lady bowed her head. "A virgin in the flesh, not the soul. My body and my life belong to Our Lord. You have forsaken the ignorant ways, have you not? Found salvation in the one true God?"

The man shrugged. "Of course. I also believe in destiny." He gestured at the agitated hounds, their anxious gaze on the lady instead of the terrified Bitty. "Your beauty befuddles the simplest of creatures, how can I resist? I envy my prey seeking refuge under your robe. It is a true miracle the hare led me directly to you. Surely fate guided the creature. It seems I am a gift from God to you, and I desire you under my protection and in my bed."

The lady frowned, and the sun fled behind a cloud. The waterfall went dull, and the blood rushed from Gwas's limbs. This would not end well for the men, he was sure of it. Nor for his friend, and he longed to hold her one last time.

Blood trickled over his ankle as he fought back the hurt and collapsed into a squat. He flung his arms out and whistled, sharp and frantic. Bitty peeked out, but the petrified traitor jerked herself back under the robe as the dogs leaped to their feet.

Their thin bodies slunk low to the ground. Ears pointed out, the dogs prowled forward. Fierce growls tore from their throats and Brochfael snapped, "Brother."

"Enough." The blue-eyed man barked at the beasts. He slapped his hand downward, cutting through the air. The hounds cringed. A few whimpers and they quieted, remaining in submissive crouches.

"Keep them controlled, Gareth, or Argo can shoot them and the stinking lad," Brochfael said. "Lady Monacella, what say you? I shall treat you like a queen."

"Nay. I told you, my flesh is bonded to the Christ."

The man grinned. "He has virgins everywhere to please him." He lost his smile and ran his fingers through his hair. "Women do not tell me no, lady. I find you attractive. Best you accept my offer."

Her grey eyes hardened, and Gwas fought his shudder. "I am not a low-born wench," she said. "God has taken me, and he protects what is his."

The bearded leader frowned. "You have driven a bitter shot to my heart. I will sweeten the proposal. I need a wife. Virtuous women of age, with hips wide for child bearing, are scarce. Marry me. I shall warm you in ways a crucified god never could."

Gwas felt the sob well in his throat. Was this man a complete idiot? Any second now, three invaders would hit the ground and clutch their pissers as they turned into snakes. Then the lady would step on them and crush them dead. She would then force him to carry them to her big iron kettle and kindle the fire.

She would offer him first bite of snake-man-stew, and then laugh when he pressed his lips tight. Her maids would gleefully howl with her. The hefty, oldest woman with hard brown eyes and a mustached lip would chase him outside, and kick him until he crawled into his burrow. *And Bitty would not be there, she would be the garnish for the meat!*

Monacella arched her brows. "The day I lose my purity is the day of my demise, and the rapist destined for hell. Be gone. Leave me to my prayers."

Gwas allowed himself a glimmer of hope. She gave these men a means of escape and only a dimwit would not attempt to flee with them. He lowered trembling fingers to the shaft, its steel point deep in his leg. He had to rescue his friend or die trying. Gwas tried to swallow the yelp jumping from his throat as an arrow thudded into the ground in front of him. He failed.

"Stop scaring him," the blue-eyed man barked at the archer and then slid off his horse.

The leader stared at the lady. "As you wish. I tire of bartering with a female, no matter how beautiful. I am no rapist, but I do require restitution for my broken heart. Saintly virgin, you shall pray for my safe-keeping and ensure I bask in the presence of God. I will deed a section of this land to you, build you a nunnery, and no man will dare to seize that which you deny me."

The smile filling Monacella's face made her features so radiant, Gwas could not stop the tears easing from under his lashes. His head ached, his leg was on fire, and he wanted to howl his rage. Never had anyone looked upon him with compassion until this younger man twisting the reins of his steed to an oak branch. The lady had beaten these powerful males to her will, and Gwas feared for them.

"Thank you, my liege," the lady simpered. "I shall pray for your soul every moment of my life, for no reason other than you are a good man. And the cost for your generosity?"

The man returned her smile. "The hare, of course."

Mighty deity who hates me, a bastard sinner, please, no. Bitty has done no wrong.

"Ahh, more than fair," the lady said. "Yet, the animal did look to me for protection." She glanced at

Gwas and terror thrilled through him. "Let God decide. Loose your hounds, and I will lift my robe to expose the vermin. After it meets its fate, you can detail your generosity to me knowing with certainty you will enjoy a bountiful life on this earth and the next."

Gwas did not have a single memory of soft female fingers soothing his hurts. If he had been held or kissed as an infant, he did not remember. He knew for a fact no one had touched him with anything other than slap or fist. The growl readying to tear from his throat contained years of pent-up fury. "That is not right. Let her go. She has done nothing to you or your bloody god. Me. Sacrifice me instead to those beasts." He shot forward.

The blow caught him beneath his ear, and he went flying up, up, and then down.

Ears ringing, blackness fought a battle for his vision. Blood trickled from his forehead, ear, and leg. It took him what seemed like forever until he could move. He blinked, shifted his face to the side, and his heart filled with hatred.

Poor Bitty dangled from the leader's large hand. This Lord Brochfael held her by the scruff of her neck, her limp body twisting.

The younger man faced the giant who had clobbered Gwas, and he strained to hear through the ringing in his ears.

"It is ill advised and foolish to risk your soul in the care of one deity. Unless you part her legs, you have but her word this nun is chaste." The man—Gareth's— voice echoed with contempt. "The hare is not the miracle." His fingers flicked toward Gwas, and he felt his throbbing jaw drop. "Look upon an abused child. Take the lad into our home, my lord. When he comes of age, a true spring offering including sacrifice will bless the fall harvest, bringing prosperity on you and any wife who will have you."

Brochfael barked a laugh. "Your counsel, dear brother, is wise." He tossed Bitty to Gareth. "Do as you think best, as will I. The woman must speak true. Otherwise, she would have joyously agreed to become queen of my chiefdom."

Who cared if a strange man wanted to shelter him? Men must hate bastards as much as women did. They would need more than a mouthful of hare to feed those hounds. Friendless and alone, there was no reason for him to try and survive this sun-blessed day.

Gwas struggled to raise himself and failed. The sight of his dead friend held securely against a firm male chest was of little comfort. The hare could not hear the big man's strong heart beating to soothe her. His own heart felt like it had died, unable to pump blood and his legs would not work. Bitty would never again nuzzle his cheek, gobble sweet strawberries from his fingers, or lay beside him on long cold nights. The darkness edging his sight widened and he sobbed. His eyelids crashed closed.

A moment later, droplets fell on his cracked lips. A huge hand slipped under his neck and effortlessly raised his head. A thick finger poked between his lips and his teeth parted. Cool water filled his mouth and he swallowed again and again. Gwas wanted to die, so why was he so thirsty? *Bitty. Is. Dead.* His throat closed, and he began to choke.

"Shh, lad." A strong hand thumped him gently on the back. "Open your eyes. Your pet's but fainted."

Seriously? He speaks true? As the soft, limp weight settled on his stomach, Gwas snapped his eyes open. Lovelier than the clear spring sky, blue eyes leaned over him. Gareth supported him to sit, and Bitty lay on Gwas's lap.

His hand shook so badly, he feared he would hurt

her. Yes, he could feel her shallow breath. A flood of emotion slammed into him. Silent tears rained off his cheeks and he clutched his friend as he gaped into the face of the man holding him.

"Come on, lad. It cannot be that bad." The man's jaw twitched. "Except my pig of a brother did give you a thump on your head and that bloody arrow must sting something terrible."

Gareth looked to the leader—his brother—speaking in low tones to the lady as the pair walked off, toward the waterfall. The archer remained standing with the horses. Gareth turned back to Gwas.

He ran his fingers along his cheek, wiped streaks of crimson on the ground, and Gwas knew then he must be dreaming. He had never had anyone touch him before, not like this, and it felt wonderful.

His tears stopped and Gwas sank, lost into the gaze of a man-angel.

"Listen," Gareth said. "Your name is no longer Gwas. I christen you...." he smiled down at Bitty. "Harey. And Harey, you are not anyone's servant. You now belong to the goddess and you are to come with me."

Me? A real name? Harey?

Gareth shifted his hand to untie a brown cloth from his waist. "Forgive me—Harey. I am placing your pet in this sack, and then I shall have to hurt you. The arrow must come out."

My name is Harey! A large hand settled over his, completely covering his own. He...Harey did not know what thrilled him more, the fact he had been deemed worthy of an identity, or the novel feel of Gareth's powerful hand sheltering him and his friend.

The man's brow furrowed. He waited for...*me, Harey!*...to release Bitty? But he wanted this moment to never end. His friend safe on his chest, and his heart stuttering with a strange emotion as Gareth's hand rose and fell, patting his shaking fingers and the hare beneath them without revulsion or violence.

"Trust me, lad. This little creature will be terrified when it wakens and sees the horse beneath us. You will not be able to calm it. You are going to faint like it did, as soon as I tug the arrow free." He lifted his hand and stared directly at Harey.

Harey opened his mouth. Nothing came out. Not even a sob. He turned his head, spat blood, and cleared his throat. "You—you won't hurt her?" he croaked.

"Never." Gareth tugged Bitty from him and tumbled the little doe into the sack. As his friend disappeared, clarity returned. Just because there was not a woman in sight did not mean the danger had passed. It never would, not as long as he breathed.

Gwas—*no, I have a name*—Harey could not give in to the black, the hurt and sorrow trying to pull him under. He had to make this wondrous man understand.

"Please." He fought the waver in his voice. "Save yourself. I beg you. Save Bitty for me. Leave me and run. Fast, before—*she*—returns." Harey sobbed at the man scrambling to his feet.

He had no words to describe the sensation flooding into his chest, cracking open his heart when Gareth's arms had wrapped around him. No matter how many hares pressed against him, deer brushed their lips on his skin, the touch of a kind human was the most amazing thing he had ever felt, but *she* would know. With one look, she would penetrate his deepest desire and understand his hope this beautiful man would ride away unscathed by his encounter with a bastard. Over and over she had told Harey he was damned. Doomed to be as immoral as the rapist who sired him, how could he take this blue-eyed angel striding for his horse to hell with him?

Gareth lashed the quiet sack containing Bitty to the horse. He tugged a glittering blade from his hip and brushed his tight woolen pants free of dirt. He then fisted the fine tunic that fell past his knees. The material had felt as soft as a fawn's skin, the weave tight and perfect. Harey gaped. He almost forgot the pain jabbing along his leg. Gareth slashed the tunic surely worth more than all the robes the lady's maids had crafted together, and approached Harey with a strip of the priceless fabric in hand.

"Gareth," the archer called out. The man—Argo—pushed off from the tree he leaned against. "You wish me to leave you to your sport? I will follow your brother. He is seeing what is involved with building a nunnery."

Gareth glanced at Argo. "Yes. Take my hounds. I will ride on ahead. God speed and do not let Brochfael jump that woman. Nor you."

Argo snickered. "Better than handling a witch's familiar. That lad is fourteen or fifteen? It is not normal that he is no bigger than a rat and runs faster than a demon."

"Sod off. He looks to have been starved. I know he outran your fat horse and hid in the trees like a fox, but he is a human in need of help, and she would not hesitate to slit your stinking throat." Gareth dropped to Harey's side. His finger under Harey's chin gave his mouth no choice but to close. He glanced to check Argo had headed off and then turned back to a dumbstruck Harey.

"Lose your fear. When you wake, you will be far from here." He dropped his hand to clasp Harey's leg above the arrow. "My apologies. The pain must be intolerable."

Harey could not believe his ears. His hand shook as

he pinched his side. Pain, yes, but did the sting shuddering through him mean he was lucid?

"We...me and Bit...my friend, are to come with you? Truly?" The air filled with dark dots and went still around him. *I am an idiot.* This man did not want an evil bastard, but maybe he would let Bitty free far away from here.

The man's eyes sparkled, his lovely face so close Harey could see every bead of sweat, and he yearned to reach out, stroke the firm lines of his cheeks. The man's smile widened and Harey felt his jaw sag.

"Shh, laddie. Yes, I am taking you away, along with the hare. I saw how that woman looked at you. I fear she will do harm the moment my back is turned."

Oh. That made sense. This kind angel-man would drop them both somewhere out of *her* reach. His heart thumped hard against his chest, and he blinked. Specks of black cleared, and he turned to follow the powerful fingers soothing down his leg, fighting the tremors shaking the limb.

Harey knew what was inside him. He had found a wooden shaft with its sharp, triangle of steel in a deer carcass before. Gareth tightened his hand on the injured thigh and happiness shivered up and down his spine. Tactile delight from the touch of a non-violent man overpowered the pain radiating from the wound. He would suffer arrows in every limb if it would prolong this moment.

"Hurts badly?" Gareth asked.

Harey drew in a deep breath and lied. "No. Thank you for helping me. I will not faint like Bitty did. I...er...you will not leave me if I can no longer run fast?"

Gareth furrowed his brow. "What? Run...." His eyes widened. "Chin up, lad, you will be riding with me. My horse can carry the three of us. Soon as we get to the castle, I will clean this wound and bind it properly. Brace yourself."

"You will hold me?" The question shot out his mouth with a nervous squeak. "On top of the big horse?" He did not care that his voice cracked, his eyes filled, and his leg burned. His lips curved into the biggest smile of his life. Then despair hit him. How could anyone be as kind as all that? He expected too much. The grin fell from his face. "Sorry. You will wrap me like Bitty and tie me on." He reached for the feathered shaft. "I-I can pull this out."

Gareth grabbed his wrist. "Are you daft? Of course I will carry you and not in a sack."

"Me?" Shock filled Harey. "In your arms?"

Confusion fled and a hot light filled the man's eyes. "That woman is a monster. Hush. I will watch over you."

Gareth's grip hardened so tight above the arrow, Harey could not help his whimper. One powerful yank, wood and steel came out, and the current of exhaustion crashing through him fought against the wave of joy flooding his heart.

Blood slithered down, dripping over his ankle. Strong fingers tied the strip of tunic around his leg and even stronger arms gathered him up. "There now. Close your eyes and rest. I will not drop you, I promise."

As lips brushed his forehead, Harey gave in to the delicious sensation branded upon his skin. His vision filled with the face of a benevolent man, and he floated into the blue darkness.

Chapter Two

Gareth could not believe how light the lad felt. The wound bled less than it should have, thanks to the lack of flesh. That fucker Argo had sunk the arrow deep enough to penetrate bone.

He shifted the unfortunate orphan under his arm and swung up onto his horse. At least the blasted hare remained quiet, as did the child. He had expected a wail or a sob when he pulled the shaft out, but the lad—Harey—showed more courage than any man Gareth had ever assisted.

He clicked his tongue, cradled his charge close, and guided the mare into a trot. The bright noon sunlight dappled through the foliage, but he lost concentration on how lovely a summer day could be. Anger fueled his thoughts.

The beautiful female, who reeked of malicious intent toward an adolescent the size of a child and his terrified little pet, had not even deemed Harey worth a name. 'Gwas' referred to a young vassal or slave. His sharp inhales, the way his eyes lit when Gareth touched him—had the boy never been held before? He had most certainly been beaten, and every time the lusty prince of Powys saw him, Brochfael would remember the woman who not only turned down a romp and then a serfdom with him, but one to whom he had given a prime section of land on impulse. No doubt he would come to resent Harey, regardless of the lad's innocence in the matter.

Gareth wished he could have rescued this starved youth before the violence and without sowing the seeds of a deceitful plan involving spring sacrifice and fall harvest. He had given in to his yearning to gather him up, carry him off to a safe haven, no matter how ill-begotten with concern to the distant future. He prayed that in the here and now he could provide a home where a young man could grow tall and strong as a lad of fifteen years should be.

Not many solutions had come to mind after he had watched arrow and then fist, strike. In order for an unwanted male to reach manhood without enduring more atrocities, Gareth needed unearthly support. Otherwise, he would not have received permission from his liege lord. Orphans were thick as vermin throughout the Roman Empire, and he had no authority over his elder brother.

Their parents dead these many years past, he had been blessed so far to survive eighteen summers. This fall he would be driven out of his brother's keep. A monastery filled with manuscripts awaited Gareth. The dogma of a solitary deity interested him, but the slaughter of non-believers as soulless infidels made as much sense as abusing a bairn because of his gender.

Even if the mother had been raped, that made the babe responsible? Unfortunately, many an ignorant lass with a fattening belly fled to the shelter of a patriarchal church, instead of embracing the renewal of life.

One thing he was sure of; he knew who a strong-willed male who outran greyhounds should serve. The goddess Eostre appreciated lust and creation. Even the dense Brochfael could comprehend a lad beloved by a creature such as the hare had to be fated for the fertility goddess.

Harey's breathing became shallow, and he cuddled closer. Long lashes occasionally fluttered and the lad snuck peeks. Gareth smiled. Harey had pulled out of his faint and pretended to sleep as he examined the man holding him.

Shifting the reins into one hand, he brushed caked blood from Harey's forehead. The deep gash would leave a scar. The lad's scrawny chest froze. Thin, hungry fingers tightened on Gareth's arm, and soft brown eyes opened. He stared up with sweet adulation.

Gareth chuckled. "Harey, I cannot believe you are conscious. How is that leg feeling?" The lad tried to lift himself, and Gareth eased him higher against his chest.

"I-I am on a horse? Where...is Bitty all right?"

"Your pet is quiet. I suspect it is as surprised as you are to be riding."

Harey blinked. His words dragged with exhaustion as he spoke, "Not it. She. Bitty is a doe. A kitten. She will miss her nest. I...my leg is fine. Thank you. I should take her back now. Should I jump free?"

"You miss your home? Do you wish to stay?"

Every muscle tensed, the thin lad shivered. "No. Not me. Bitty. I can relocate the warren, before...well, I hid them but surely her family is at risk because of me."

Gareth tightened his grip. "No. I will not allow it. Regardless of their fate, you are not returning anywhere near a future nunnery. Bitty must find new relatives in a new home, just like you. Would you like to hold the reins?"

Harey's eyes grew so wide, a laugh burst from Gareth, and he slowed the mare. Gently as he could, he swung him up and around so he mounted the horse in front of him. He loosened his arms, tugged Harey's limp fingers to take the reins, and clucked the horse onward.

To his astonishment, the mare twisted her head to nicker up at Harey and the lad giggled. "She likes me!"

"I see that. You have a way with four-legged creatures."

"And you? My body close to you...will you be damned into eternal fires as well? I fear *she* will pray to the Christ, and bad things will happen. I...beg your pardon, but do you not understand what awaits a bastard such as me?"

"Harey, even if hell exists, I do not care, and I also do not give a rat's arse who sired you, in or out of wedlock. I like holding you. Best get used to it. What other nonsense did those women teach you?"

"Teach me? Er...nothing." Harey took a deep breath. "But I hide and listen and remember. Never before you did I see big men up close. In the summers, I heard fierce wolf dogs." The nervous lad averted his gaze as he hardened the tremble from his voice. "Men had to have been nearby, but I do not know what happened to them. Snakes and rats scurry beneath the huts. If you let me and Bitty go, maybe you will not fall under a spell. I fear you so tiny with the four legs of a rat, or none at all like a snake. Release me, I beg you. Please?"

"Nay. Cease asking." Gareth nuzzled the top of Harey's head with his chin. "Listen, witches are not real. The lady Monacella is strange and cruel, yes, but only a woman and one whom you no longer serve. Everyone has a destiny, and I will see to it you fulfill yours with joy in your heart." He placed his hand above the lad's on the reins. "Stop worrying and rest. We have another good hour's ride. I give my word. You are safe, and so am I."

The lad's jaw sagged. "I-I thought you lied to make me sleep. You are really taking *me*—" His thin voice cracked. "—to your home?"

Gareth ached to wrap his hands round a nun's neck. "I will say it as often as you would like, laddie. The woman you fear to be a witch is not your keeper. I am. A shaft deep in the flesh saps a man's strength. Sleep a bit longer and then you can really hold these reins, and I will get a chance to snore."

A soft snort of amazement and then a short sigh eased from Harey's lips. "But I don't want...."

"Yes?"

"If I sleep...perchance you will not be holding me when I wake."

Gareth chuckled. "You have my word. I shall not desert you. Let me explain what will happen to a lad who saved a young hare, took an arrow, escaped a den of men-haters, and rode a mighty steed. Upon arrival at his new home, he will heal in a hot bath. Wounds cleaned, stomach filled with delicious foods, he shall rest with arms around him for as long as he wants. The leveret, too."

He soothed Harey into sleep, and the ride passed as guilt and worry weaved in and out of his thoughts. What type of man branded another with the mark of a sacrifice for a pagan goddess? Easy answer—a desperate one. Idiot that he was, he would do his best to ensure this particular lamb would not be threatened with the knife for many moons yet. He would work the idea into his brother's dense skull that a tall, plump male with the shadow of whiskers on his face would better please a lusty, fun-loving goddess than a youthful bundle of skin and bones.

Finally, the clouds within his mind parted and his heartbeat jumped as he rounded the curve to trot alongside the fields in front of his brother's stone fortress. As he neared the village, two beloved maidens raced out of the third hut down.

"Gareth!" Maura's sweet voice trilled. "What a lovely surprise. And whom have you brought us?"

She wore a white shift that barely reached her knees. Thin straps of blue linen crossed and supported her breasts, and the hot flame in her green eyes sent jolts of lust south to curl his toes.

He could not dwell on the curves of a beauteous woman. Harey had stiffened the moment Maura spoke. His soft brown eyes fluttered open, wide with apprehension. Gareth could not help himself. He smacked a kiss on the lad's forehead, tightened his arms, and smiled at the eldest Landy sister.

"My love, this orphan needs a bath and food before I present him to Lord Brochfael." He traced soothing circles on Harey's arm. "Harey, the gorgeous lady in white is Maura, sister to Davina."

Harey remained frozen. His gaze fastened on Maura, his expression mirrored the one of a wounded deer. Anger galloped up and down Gareth's spine. "Shh, lad. I will not let go of you before you are ready. These lasses are not to be feared."

Gareth sighed. Maura lost her smile, but her kind face filling with concern did not deter the lad trying to merge his bones into Gareth's. He could feel Harey's heart struggling to crack open his chest and flee, far and fast.

"Oh! Oh!"

Harey jerked to stare down at the tiny lass squeaking with outrage as she patted Gareth's foot.

"Gareth! There's blood! On his poor toes. Can I touch his leg? I want to clean him."

"Not yet, Vina. He is frightened, hurt, and hungry."

Gareth grinned as little sister tossed her brown

curls and glared at big sister. "Fetch a lot of water. Maybe the entire creek. There is much blood. I smelled bread at Owen's. Steal all of it."

Harey twisted to gawk at Gareth. "That is a lass? A baby?"

"Whaat! I am not a bairn. I am five years of age. Why is part of Gareth's tunic wrapped around your leg?" Vina smacked Gareth again. "Will his leg turn rotten and fall off? Is bone sticking out? Can you fix him?"

"Hush, Vina," Maura said. "Gareth, bring him inside."

Gareth nodded at Maura and handed Vina the reins. Her rosebud mouth formed a circle of surprise, and her delighted gasp got a twitch from Harey's lips. Unfortunately, his slender frame tightened, muscles readied to try and pull loose of Gareth's grip as big sister hurried to help.

"I said, shhh. Relax." Gareth lifted him, swung his leg around and dropped to his feet. Harey clung, threatening to cut off the blood flow in Gareth's arm. A gulp for courage and then a low whistle burst from Harey. Gareth halted. He had forgotten the blasted hare.

Maura gasped. "That sack is moving."

A deep shudder shook the lad. "Do not hurt her." He tugged at Gareth. "Put me down? I am not hungry. My leg is fine. Please?"

"Not going to happen, lad. You are off the leg until I dress it with salve to fight infection. Maura, there is a leveret in there. Let her hop out. Do not scare her, right, lass? Vina, can you manage the knot?"

Maura's nimble fingers jumped to help. Their smiles filled Gareth's heart as Vina squealed with delight when the little creature leaped free. The hare reversed direction in mid-air and fell to land on her feet. A frantic glance at Vina and the hare's muscles locked in place.

"Bitty, I am way up here." Harey groaned and the animal spun her head around. "The big man will not put me down. He pledged he would not harm you. Come to us."

Encouraged by the lad's soft clucks, the hare hopped right up to Gareth. He squatted, Bitty leaped into Harey's hands, and Gareth straightened. Two gleeful lasses clapped their hands and the color rose in Harey's cheeks. He shook like a leaf tumbling in the winds of 'what's happening to me.'

In the bustle of feminine activity to come, Harey held tight to his pet. He darted worried peeks at Maura and looked around the thatched hut like it was a castle.

Water heating, Maura blinked back tears when Harey refused the bread before he had offered a bite to his hare. When she approached with hot broth to dunk the crust in, Gareth held the bowl and chuckled as Harey's eyes went wide and he gobbled at the sopped chunk. He licked his lips, his thin face all scrunched while his gaze flickered between the loaf in Maura's hand, and his pet eating the last of the piece in his own. When Vina came running in clutching sweet clover and a clump of radishes, the hare squirmed.

"Let Bitty hop down." Gareth stroked Harey's arm. "Vina will watch her. Look. See what Maura has scavenged for you, fresh from the hearth." The charred pheasant leg smelled sweet and ripe and Gareth's stomach growled.

Maura halted as the lad began shaking. The frozen deer look again filled his face and he pressed into Gareth. "Harey?" he whispered.

The lad tore his gaze from the hare chomping the radish Vina held by its leaf. "No, thank you. I-I am very full. Did-did I say thank you?"

"But you only had some bread," Gareth said. "You do not like meat?"

"I never ate it before." Harey drew a shaky breath and spoke to the ground. "Smells like...stew for the seventh day. Sometimes hooded, big...maybe men brought supplies. I looked and counted and searched everywhere, but I do not think they all left. Most times, I was not allowed inside. I wanted to help them, but I am not a good person, I—I am a coward. Do you wish me to leave?"

Gareth scoffed. "Stop that. You are not going anywhere. Forget the past. I have laid claim to you." A neglected lad's imagination must have run wild. Gareth swallowed his snarl and patted Harey's thigh. "It is a pheasant leg, but we should keep the fare simple until you are stronger." He winked at Maura and then widened his grin for Harey. "No one eats of a man here except in a very pleasurable way without any loss of flesh."

"Gareth!" Maura dropped the meat back by the hearth and smacked Gareth on the head with the bread. She ignored Harey's flinch, tossed the loaf in his lap, and headed for the door. "Vina, if you can get a radish from Bitty, Harey might like one. You ever have a radish, Harey?"

The lad did not answer, his mouth filled with the chunk of bread Gareth had shoved against his lips. By the way his eyes lit after he had swallowed and Gareth popped the tart vegetable into his mouth, he knew radishes were a success.

Two bowls of broth, six radishes, and half a loaf of bread later, Gareth shifted him off his knee. One hand around the lad's waist, he made to remove the threadbare tunic.

Harey darted his gaze at Maura beside the fire. She smiled, her eyes bright, and dumped another bucket of heated water into the wood tub. Gareth returned her smile. "We will need some salve. Clean strips of linen also. I shall replace your supplies once I have been to the castle."

She nodded. "Vina, run fetch clothing. The O'Malleys lost their lad. They will have a clean tunic to spare."

The child gave Bitty one last pat and scrambled to her feet. "Maybe there are some carrots in their garden, too." She skipped out the door.

"Bathe inside?" Harey whispered. "But I heard water beyond the trees alongside the cleared chunks of land. May I jump in the creek? Please?"

"Warm water feels wonderful." Gareth brushed long, tangled hair over Harey's shoulder.

Harey straightened his thin frame. He inched aside as he gulped. "Warm, not boiling?"

Gareth barked a laugh. "You are so daft, lad. We will not cook you. Just make you feel good."

"Oh." Harey's mouth hung open. He stared at Gareth with that adoring pup look and grasped his tunic. Gareth hastened to help him. Tattered and rough, blood stained the linen everywhere. It appeared the boy had used his teeth to chew a tunic short, so it fell below his knees and did not impede him when he fled evil nuns. Gareth tossed it to Maura. She allowed it to fall at her feet. Her jaw dropped and eyes blazed hot. He jerked his head to follow her gaze. She stared at numerous, thin scars crisscrossing the scrawny back, buttocks and thighs.

Harey shuddered, hunching his shoulders to appear as small as he could. His cheeks crimson, he turned stiff as an oak waiting for the axe to strike. He shook ragged hair to hide his face, dropped his hands to cover his sex, and examined his feet.

Rage pumping hot and heavy inside him, Gareth

squatted next to him. "Stop that, lad. It is only the welt marks. Maura has never seen such abuse before. Neither have I." He fought the urge to brush his fingers along the deep welts. *Best concentrate on current atrocities.* He carefully reached to tug Harey's hand free, placed it on his shoulder, and untied the linen strip from around his injured leg.

Crusted with dark blood, the wound looked angry, but no fresh seepage. Gareth scooped him up, crossed to the hearth, and lowered him into the tub.

"The water too hot?"

Harey's shy smile and his soft exhale told him otherwise.

The moment Vina returned, Maura whispered at her and shooed her out again. She shared a bemused glance with Gareth while Harey sank down into the water. Soft, mud-colored eyes widened, bright and amazed as the lad's body went limp and pleasure eased the stress from his face.

Vina raced back into the hut, hand in hand with Owen, her excited eight-year-old friend.

Owen needed no persuasion to strip and climb in. Close to the same size as the malnourished Harey, both lads fit in the tub like peas in a pod. Any remnants of tension dissipated as Owen chattered and examined the wounds and scars with astonished innocence.

Maura and Gareth exchanged grievous looks. Harey's spellbound stare made it clear he had never seen another child before this day, let alone been touched and inspected by one. Owen's tiny fingers patted blood away from Harey's shins while Gareth tackled the lad's forehead.

When Maura approached with soap, Harey drew his legs up, his toes connected with Owen's. He did not even flinch while she washed the child's hair, his face bright as Owen shrieked with laughter when Maura tickled his ribs and kissed him.

After Vina dumped Bitty on top of the lads, Gareth swooped in with his knife and trimmed long matted hair until brown tendrils brushed Harey's shoulders, while Owen tormented the soaked hare. Harey's heavy-lidded eyes crinkled with bliss. Gareth soaped and massaged, trailing his fingers until blood and dirt eased from the lad's hair and scalp.

Soon two were sparkling clean, dried, and dressed, and Vina splashed in the tub. Maura sent Owen home with promises he could teach Harey to skip rocks come the morrow.

Gareth laid Harey flat on Maura's straw mattress and dressed and bound the wound. He stroked, kneading the stress from astonishingly muscular limbs as the lad cuddled his pet. Skin and bones, he had kept pace with a terrified hare and surely could outrun any man. It did not take long before a wide yawn split his thin face.

"Not yet. Before you sleep, we must do something about Bitty."

All trace of weariness fled Harey's expression. "What is wrong with her?"

"Not a thing." Gareth smiled. "The villagers and vassals need to meet her. I will slap some sense into the hounds. Cannot have them chasing after the pair of you again. You would leave them dead of exhaustion behind you."

"But I fear she shall not understand anything other than sharp teeth. How can...will you protect her?"

"Everyone will. This is her home. Our mighty lord and his fat archer will have returned, and I shall mark your pet as safe." Gareth gathered Harey and Bitty into his arms and winked. "Unless they have been turned into toads, of course." He snickered as Harey gulped.

"Stop teasing him," Maura snapped. "Toads or not,

your bloody brother's dark castle is not a fit place. He needs much attention and care. Three years younger than you and he is the size of a child? His back. His leg. I do not want Argo or that sod Colin near him. I wish him to stay here."

"Gareth?" Harey's clutch grew desperate.

He shifted the lad tighter. "No one will again raise a hand to him. Now he is with us, Harey will thrive and grow to his potential, no matter the harvest, sickness, or war. It is fated."

That was assuming his suck-arse plan worked. He strode to exit the smoky hut. "Maura, love, tell everyone to gather in the bailey before sunset."

Outside, he nodded to the people already grouping, patted Harey's thigh, and headed for the mare.

Chapter Three

*T*he sun sank low, and Gareth's forearm began to throb. He feared Harey was lighter than any abused orphan in all of Briton, but he had dug his nails in and Gareth had not the heart to pry him loose. Quiet as the hare cuddled into his chest, Harey stared at every inch of the stone fortress. He flinched from the curious gaze of the wenches cleaning the kettles, stroking the fires in the kitchen area and stiffened when Gareth carted him into the great hall.

In the cluster of rowdy men, Broch and Argo sat at the head of the long wood table, the stirring hounds at their feet. Guffaws and whistles followed Gareth's heels as he came to a halt and faced his brother. Harey ducked his head and pressed as tightly as he could into Gareth.

"Toss the leveret to Arturo." Argo raised his slopping goblet. "Your lead hound hunted well." He sneered at the quivering lad. "What plans have ye for that runt? He is scarcely a mouthful for the dogs either."

"Shut your mouth, Argo," Gareth snapped. "Stay." A sharp cluck and the excited dogs froze, trembling as they stared at the hare under Harey's arm.

Broch wiped the grease from his lips onto his sleeve and tossed his hunk of mutton onto the table. He arched his brows at Gareth. "Yes, 'twas a fine hunt this morn. The lady Monacella will wither on her knees, marking my passage into heaven. One month hence, you will pray for me also. When you're joined with God, I do not want your leavings underfoot. Get him out of here. Toss him in the stables."

Gareth scowled. "Brother, don't be a tarse." Smirks around the table disappeared as the lord's eyebrows snapped downward. Gareth needed to distract the bod-head fast, before Broch clobbered him and Harey across the courtyard. He raised his chin. "I request audience to introduce Eostre's choice. The serfs are gathering. Your permission, I will speak from my balcony with you beside me."

Gareth turned to Harey, patted him, and then tugged him loose. "You need to greet my hounds. I will hold Bitty." He left no choice. He set him on his feet, forced the leveret from him, and pushed him to stand alone. Gareth clicked his tongue. "Gitta, Arturo, Bowden, Enid—come."

The dogs bounded forward, teeth bared in drooling grins. Gareth held snug to the little hare. He could feel its heart yammering to explode. Arturo dipped his head, the other three hounds tripping over each other behind him. Hindquarters rose in the air, tails wagged so hard he wondered who would fall over first, the hounds or the trembling lad.

"Gareth?" Not a drop of blood in his cheeks, Harey looked up at him.

"Do not make them beg too long. Pet them."

"I-I never touched a wolfhound before." Fingers shaking, he inched forward.

Despite Gareth's growl, Bowden could take it no longer. She lurched forward, knocking her head into

Harey's stomach as Arturo sprang to smack his drooling tongue along his cheek. Harey's gasp, his gulp of surprise brought grins all around. Broch, stiff tarse that he was, twitched his lips and snorted.

Harey dug his fingers into thick grey fur and pushed Bowden aside. His eyes bright, he patted his hand from one whimpering head to the next.

Gareth squatted and Arturo poked his snout into the frozen hare. His arm around Bowden's neck, Harey shook like a petrified mother hen. Arturo sniffed the hare, twisted up to lick Gareth's cheek, and spun around to knock into Bowden and take her place beside Harey. The heat rising in the lad's face as each hound made the hare welcome filled Gareth's heart. When the men burst into applause, Harey beamed as if he had swallowed the sun.

Gareth straightened and handed the hare to Harey. "Now 'tis time to meet your human friends." He scooped the boy up and jerked his chin at Broch. "Send your vassals into the courtyard and join me in my room." He clicked for the hounds to follow and strode past rowdy, noisy louts.

"Gareth? What is a tarse?" Harey whispered and snuggled into his chest.

"A bod, cock, what dangles between our legs. But do not say the word to Brochfael. He will strangle you."

Harey shivered. "I regret he does not like me. I want to piss when he looks at me, but he is not as scary as...*she* was."

Gareth bounded up the rough stone steps. "Most often, Broch strives to be a moral man. Not even close to being as misguided as that woman. Once his brain starts functioning, he will appreciate what you have to offer." A soft chuckle escaped Gareth's lips. "Even Bitty is more intelligent than my brother, but he will come around to accept you both. I swear to make certain you grow as strong as any man so you have no need to fear their fists. I know you have reason to be leery of women, but you will learn otherwise with them as well. You must. You belong to a goddess."

"G-goddess? Can I not belong...to you?"

"Shh. Do you like my bedroom?"

He twisted his blank stare from Gareth. His gaze darted from the thatched reeds underfoot, the flickering of the fire, to the large, four-post bed. He took in the raised platform with a log seat, and the priceless parchment strewn about beside the feathered pen.

"You make markings? *She*...er...the lady did too. Is it magic? Crafted to this goddess?"

"No. Only a means of communication which I could teach you."

"Teach...me?" Harey gulped. "I would like that." He flushed. "I would more than like that, it...this must be what heaven is like. I hope a goddess does not learn a bastard has been taken to paradise."

His little face glowed up at Gareth, and he felt his heart crack. He was an arse, and this lad deserved better. But again, what else could he do?

"There now. Call yourself ill begotten again—I will turn you over to Maura to tickle to death. Dear lad, forget the goddess. Don't listen to a word I am about to say, just smile for your new friends. These people are good. They shall come to love you, I promise."

And if man or woman lays a finger on you, forces you to their will, I will gut them.

The bustle of two hundred plus gathered outside filtered in the window. Gareth dropped a kiss on top of Harey's head and crossed the room, the hounds snapping at his heels. He kicked aside the screen and stepped out onto the balcony. He halted in front of the foot high slab of square stone framing the balcony's edge and stroked Harey's arm. The lad shivered at the boisterous group twenty feet below. As soon as Broch's large frame loomed behind them, a hush fell upon the populace.

Gareth cleared his throat and projected his voice. "One lunar cycle has passed since the light of day equaled the dark of night. This night, the full moon of Ostara will rise. This night, we sow the seeds—choice foods, soft clothing, loving arms—to fatten our future. This night, begins years of teaching, sheltering and protecting a chosen one."

Gareth hefted Harey high and shouted, "Praise to Eostre! Praise to the hare! Welcome to Eostre's hare!"

"Huh?" the monster of a bearded male bellowed from the front. A head taller than any other, Patrick held his youngest, Owen, perched on his shoulders. He barked up at Gareth, "I shall kick your arse. Speak plain, you pagan sod. He is a spring offering? For the goddess?"

"Yes, idiot," he bellowed back. "His name is Harey, and he must not only reach manhood first, he has to thrive and learn to master letters and numbers. We shall teach him everything we know. That would be nothing from you, Patrick Conald. We must care for him above all others. No man should raise a hand to him or force him to his knees. He is to remain a virgin, pure as freshly fallen snow. And no women can fawn over him, until he loses his fear. Anyone who does otherwise will face my sword. What say you all to that, my friends?"

"The lad—Harey—is everyone's bairn to love." Patrick turned to the crowd. "Hail to Eostre's Hare!"

"Harey! Harey! Harey!" the mob chanted.

Broch stepped forward. "Release the hare and the lad, Gareth. Commit to Eostre. With the one Father granting me long life, your gwas will be safe until his beard fills in. If this hare pleases the pagans, and the nun prays to Rome, both religions should bring prosperity. Throw the pair to the winds and we shall see who claims them—or who eats them."

Gareth gritted his teeth. His arsehole of a brother wanted another sign. Stomach knotted with tension, Gareth bent to Harey's ear and lied. "Drop Bitty. She will be fine." He snapped his fingers at the bloody hounds milling behind Broch. "Down. Stay." They snarled and fell.

His huge eyes fevered with astonishment, Harey stared at Gareth. He nodded.

"Sorry, Bit. He said...Gareth vowed you to be safe." Harey eased the hare out of his hands and she fell to her feet and hopped to huddle by Gareth's foot. To his relief, jaws less than four feet away snapped and grumbled, but stayed put.

"And now the gwas," Brochfael said.

"His name is Harey, you tight arse." Gareth bit his lip and forced a smile for the lad. "It is your turn to fly free of my arms. Let your family hold you." He raised his head and called out, "Patrick, give Owen his feet and step forward. Open your arms for our future."

"Gareth?" Harey squeaked.

"I shall be right here." Gareth kissed his forehead and lifted him as he yelled, "When Eostre's hare grows strong as the wolf, tall as the pines, virile as the horned stag, blessings will be ours to reap." His stomach churning, he forced trembling arms from around his neck and flung the lad into the crowd.

The hare sprang before Patrick clasped Harey in the hug of a massive bear. With a spectacular leap, she bounded up and over the edge. Their instinct to chase strong, the hounds yelped and lunged.

Gareth lurched to tackle Arturo. "Heel," he snapped. "Broch! Get Bowden. She will break her damn neck."

Brochfael kicked out and three hounds twisted and then scrambled past him to race through the bedroom. Gareth released Arturo. He stood and hid the surge of relief, his wobbling legs from his brother.

Surrounded by cooing women, men patted any spot of Harey they could reach, and Patrick roared with laughter at the hare butting into his foot. Harey flung his arm out, and as Patrick dipped, the leveret hopped. The hare smacked into Patrick's broad chest and burrowed herself under Harey's arm.

Owen hung onto Patrick's thigh and punched at anyone coming close to the lad's injured leg, including the hounds that had burst out the castle's entrance to join the melee.

Broch's heavy hand landed on Gareth's shoulder. Gareth grabbed his brother's arm to lift it high. "Hail to the lord of Powys!"

"Brochfael! Brochfael!" The cheers rang out.

Amidst all the laughter and the mauling of Harey, Gareth saw that Maura stood apart. Her hand wrapped around Vina's, her hard stare drilled into him. Throwing a starved runt into Patrick's capable hands would not get her riled. But promising to revive pagan rites? So much for a lusty goddess blessing Gareth this night. After the moon rose, he would have a tough time parting any legs but his own.

How many answers did a third son have? Da had died in war. Mamai died with a stillborn sister. Grief held hands with self-loathing within him. His beloved brother closest in age had fallen in a hunting accident. He had no one but Maura and her sister to cherish for the past year.

He hardened his will. He had done the right thing. Times were harsh and cruel. Few survived so parent could hold a bairn on their knee, no matter what deity they bowed to. He would fade away in a monastery, Colin—ugly sod of a brother to Argo—would place a ring on Maura's finger, and a lonely orphan would have some semblance of a happy adolescence.

Waves of red colored the sky as the sun kissed the horizon. Gareth jerked his gaze from the angry lass. His heart floundered. Even from up here he could see Harey's grip on Patrick had not lessened, and the lad squirmed, looking for Gareth. He had better go take him back. He would wait until his charge slept deep, and then cross the fields and pray for the sake of his aching loins his love forgave him, stupid man that he was.

He heaved a sigh and turned to his brother. "Thank you for taking in Harey and his pet. I will see to it he learns respect and obedience—and how to draw a bow. He owes that arse Argo one."

Brochfael chuckled. "Argo did miss the heart. That's more than I can say for you. Your little tick has latched on. He will suck you dry if you let him."

Gareth snorted and stomped past his laughing brother.

It took him well past dusk to lull an exhausted Harey to close his eyes. Overwrought at being indoors and covered with soft furs, the lad finally drifted off, the hare pressed against his leg.

Gareth eased him from his shoulder. He slipped out of his bedroom, plundered the kitchens, and ran for his mare.

 C8

Maura slapped him. Hard enough to knock him from her mattress.

"Why? You know your horrid brother will see to it blood actually spills."

44

"Many things can happen in one year, let alone two or three." Gareth rubbed his jaw and ogled. Her hair tumbled free of her braids, soft and lovely in the pale light of a plump moon. Full breasts strained against the tunic and he stood his ground. As long as she did not aim low, there was chance of gaining entry to heaven.

"Oh, Gareth, it is not fair. You are leaving us soon. If I had the heart to abandon my sister like my da did, run off and read books all day, I would want to. I wish I were not a woman and not good enough for the one god. But, you stupid lout, a sacrifice to a bloodthirsty goddess?" Fury filled her eyes and her fist rose.

He grasped her wrist. "I am grateful to any deity that you are a woman. Forget my sins for this night. Please, love?" He released her and eased back, ready to bolt if her heated gaze did not head south to take note of the desperate state he was in.

Hotter and happier than butterflies, visions of his fair maid danced inside his head, strumming down into his stomach in the direction of a cock stiffer than any maypole in existence. He throbbed, sap dribbled from the thin slit, and he feared he would soon stain his tunic. She had known he would come to her bed. Vina must be sharing Owen's nest, which meant big sister would yield to him. Eventually.

"I hate you. Bastard. Make sure you pull out in time." Maura wrenched free and flung her hand around his neck. "I will embrace an abused lad, but a wee bairn in my stomach means I will come to this abbey after you with an axe. Kiss me."

He took her lips and showed his delight with his tongue. Lust tightened his balls into rocks, as the taste of her filled him. How he loved kissing Maura. Almost as much as he enjoyed slipping his hand up and under her tunic. Soft curly hairs wrapped around his fingers, and she moaned into his mouth.

Fingers hunting for the sweet moist opening, he plunged and explored her mouth as he pushed her backward to the mattress. There. The entrance to heaven. He curled his finger inside to tease and caress her wider, fit for a thick cock and Maura eased aside. Gasping, she tumbled flat. Garth followed her, and promised his fingers they would soon return despite his cock howling in outrage. She liked to be cuddled and made ready, and he yearned to please her. He used both hands to tug her tunic over her head.

"I love you, Maura. I wish I could be your husband, but this moment will last in my heart forever." He yanked his tunic off, tossed it, and thanked the goddess he had left his woolen pants at the castle.

The sight of her nude body glistened in the soft light and imprinted on his memory. So beautiful, her lips softly open. Gareth loomed over her and parted her thighs. This time he slid and twisted two long fingers into her, while his thumb brushed her hot spot. He cupped one full breast and lowered his lips for the other.

"Gareth. Stop." Her fist punched his shoulder. "Now."

What? Please, please, no. Why? He trailed his fingers out of Maura and twisted to follow her line of sight past his shoulder.

Bloody hell. The outline of a small lad, his head bowed, stood a few feet away.

"What the fuck—"

The smack of Maura's hand slapping Gareth's arse coincided with a soft sob.

Harey turned to flee. Gareth tumbled off his lass, aided by Maura's sharp shove. He found his feet and snapped, "Harey. No." He hardened his voice. "Don't you dare run. If I have to hunt—best not make me angry, lad!" He grabbed his tunic, pulled it on and charged. Outside the hut, he lunged past a hopping leveret and grabbed the youth with shoulders slumped, shaking with despair like a cornered hart.

Another strangled sob and Gareth's cock went whoosh, soft and twitching with depression. "Shh. I beg forgiveness. I did not mean to yell at you." An arm flung under the knees gave the lad little choice as Gareth gathered up and carried him back inside. He choked back his groan as lovely breasts disappeared under Maura's tunic. He set Harey on the edge of the bed and dropped to his knees in front of him. "I cannot believe you crossed the fields on that leg. What is amiss?"

"You...." Harey hunched into himself, twisted his hands together and stared at Gareth's chest.

His finger under the lad's chin forced him to raise his gaze. The silver moonlight could not hide the streaks of tears on his thin face. "I told you I would not leave you and I lied. I am sorry. My plan was to return before you woke."

Maura shifted to the farthest corner of the straw mattress. "Forget Brochfael's dank castle. You are staying here. We have a treat for you come sunrise. Have you ever had an egg before?"

Gareth grinned down at him. "Oh yes. Only special lads get to eat eggs. They are a heavenly gift. The more a bairn gets of them, the taller they grow. I stole five out from under Argo's nose. All for you."

Harey sniffed and wiped his face with the back of his hand. "Sparrow eggs? Like the ladies love to eat?"

Gareth swung himself into the comfort of Maura's bed and reached for Harey. "Nah. Not the wee ones only fit for insane witches. There are these rare birds. A new breed, hatched from a pheasant and an ostrich, I think. They lay the most delicious, huge eggs."

"Ostrich?"

"A giant winged myth, bigger than you, that nests far across the sea. Argo plundered hens and a cock from the Vikings who stole them from the Franks of Gaul. He has been breeding them this past year."

"Franks?"

"A land where cocks roam free. Men sleep with men and women—"

"Gareth!" Maura punched him.

"Will not Argo be angered?" Harey asked.

Gareth settled his arm over the lad's scrawny shoulder. "He is ignorant. Cannot count. I raid his stash all the time. If you tell him, he will aim an arrow at my head and then hit my leg."

Harey wrapped his fingers around Gareth's wrist. "I will bite his hand off first."

Maura spooned against his back, Harey molded into his chest, the bloody hare pressed against his foot, and Gareth thought his heart would overflow with warmth.

Chapter Four

*M*aura basked in the warmth shining down upon her and fought the sob welling in her chest. A river of misery flooded her stomach. It was not a simple matter to hide her grief when the sun shone so strong, and corn and wheat grew plump and perfect, encouraging the villagers to crow with joy. Unfortunately, the bloody daylight would not cease disappearing beneath the horizon. Endless night would be fine with her, but morn kept returning, leaving her aching to hold tight to the man who would be gone on the morrow.

She stared at Gareth, muscles rippling in his broad back. Her gaze lingered on his tapered waist and sweet arse as he showed Harey how to swing the axe and stack winter's wood so the rain slipped though faster. She hovered around the corner of the hut and swallowed back drool as she tore her sights from the backside of her lover to the small form beside him.

She was not alone in fighting panic, unable to figure out how to make the sun freeze in the sky and time to stand still. Six weeks since he had taken his first indoor bath, and the lad still flinched when he spoke to Maura. He never addressed her first, and sometimes she caught him peeking at her with amazement as if he could not wrap his mind around the fact she enjoyed his presence.

The poor lad continued to jump out of his skin at sudden movements from anyone other than Gareth. She suspected Harey feared the moment his protector was not near, the women in this village would grasp leather and add to the cruel welts marking every inch of his back and buttocks. The lad slowed his pace to match Gareth's every footstep. His thin face puckered with worry whenever the man attempted to lose his little shadow.

Maura sighed. She shifted her basket, heavy with fat potatoes, ears of corn, long thick carrots, from hip to arm and approached.

"Greetings, love." Gareth slung the axe to notch into the stump and beamed at Maura as he smacked the dust from his hands. "Give your gatherings to Harey." He grinned at the frowning lad who was busy tossing splintered pine onto the tallest heap of firewood in all of Briton. "Come on, you know you are a better cook than she is. I need to...take a walk. We shall not be gone but an hour or so."

"I cannot come with you?" Harey blinked. Long lashes fluttered with longing, more pretty than any lass's, and Maura felt her heart clench. "Please," he whispered. "Let me swim in the creek with you...and her, right?"

Harey's streaked tunic stuck to his shrunken chest. Six weeks of shoving any bit of fat he would accept at him, and the lad who loved his carrots still looked the size of a child. His legs had grown, though. He had shot up an amazing couple of inches. A healthy bead of sweat dripped, twisting past the scar on his forehead where bloody Brochfael had cracked his skin open.

Gareth turned his pleading gaze upon her while Harey lowered his to stare at his toes. She hastened to shove the basket at Gareth. "Put this on the table and let us pray Bitty leaves us some scraps."

"As you wish." He grasped the blessings of the fields and grinned. The big lout did not want anyone around on this particular swim, Gareth's last chance to lie on top of her until spring thawed bleak winter from the isle. He headed for the hut, Harey scampering on his heels.

"Harey, wait."

Gareth did as well. "Yes, dear lady?"

"Nothing. Go away," Maura commanded him.

Harey slumped, turning back as Gareth shrugged and strode for the door.

She sighed. "I only want a word with you."

His apprehensive gaze slowly rose. Large eyes, the color of overturned sod, fastened on her and then submissively lowered.

"You are hot and sticky," she said. "Of course you may jump in the creek with Gareth, but Harey? Talk to me. Are you worried what shall happen when he leaves?"

She watched the ball in his throat bob.

"Yes," he whispered, his voice a nervous croak.

"He will only be gone until the snow melts. You may sleep in the big bed with Vina and me, on the floor, or with Owen. If you disobey and run off, I shall have to get Patrick and come after you. If our mighty Brochfael refuses us a pair of horses to do so, well, it is a hand lost for stealing bread, but horse thieves dangle from a rope. At the risk of our lives, Harey, you must not go after him. I am sorry."

"Why will you not make him stay?" he blurted. He jerked his chin up to stare past her and Maura followed his gaze.

"Fetch clean tunics," she called to Gareth watching them from the doorway, "the pair of you swim while I prepare our repast."

"No, lass. I want you in that creek. Harey—"

"Gareth." Maura stomped her foot. "Give us a moment. If you ever *want* me anywhere again, you will do as I ask."

The love of her life scowled, muttering as he ducked back inside.

"Gareth has told you repeatedly women, orphans, youngest sons have few options. I know he has asked you to watch over me and Vina, but we will be fine on our own."

Harey's chest heaved and his chin dropped.

"We need you here because this is your home and we love you. Once you reach manhood, you can do as you please. Even bypass the monastery to head for an improper den of women."

His head reared up. "I am supposed to return to...her? The nuns?"

For the first time she saw the man this lad could grow to become. A hard edge to his expression, his sights directly on her and she wanted to bite her tongue.

"No, no," she said. "Those women are pure evil. I meant, well, there are places men go to find companionship for pleasure. Forget my blunder. I am trying to explain that in this summer of your life, you are as fated as I am to be left behind, under our protection, until Gareth returns."

"I do not understand. He wishes to be with men. To study at this monastery." Harey wilted back into a confused and frightened child, the whine clear in his tones. "Why does he not think I am man enough to be a man with him? If I vowed to be a follower, sought out and begged the Baptist to wash the sins of a bastard from me, they still will not allow me there?"

"Harey." Maura made her tones as gentle as she could. "You are not yet a man. You must stay here in the village until you are."

"You are lying." He scowled as he shuffled his foot in the dirt. "I am to be kept with women and bairns and get fatter, so I can serve a goddess." He thrust his lower lip out. "Please. I like books, writing, and big men. I will be good, I promise."

"No, you will not," Gareth's deep voice spoke past Maura's shoulder. She turned to glower at him.

His gaze stayed locked on Harey. "A bad lad destined for trouble, you will rest in my place here and in my bed at the castle. Maura and Patrick will see to it big men keep their sodding hands off you. You will steal every egg you can, pull Vina's braids, throw rocks at a bod-head's castle, play all the day with Owen, put creepy things in the huts of the lass or woman who dares touch you, punch any fucker—"

"Gareth!" Maura rolled her eyes.

Harey crossed his arms over his chest. "When will I be big enough for Eostre..." his voice cracked, "and for you, Gareth?"

"I will show you. Stand where you are until I say otherwise." Gareth started toward the forest. "The day you can take a man down is the day you answer to no one but the gods."

He stopped thirty feet away and faced them. His stance wide, he flung his arms out.

Harey's face creased with worry and Maura yearned to gather him to her breast.

"Come on, you little runt," Gareth barked. "Become king of the castle."

Before she could blink, in a burst of speed that defied human limbs, Harey shot forward. His leap barreled him into Gareth's chest.

Not even a stumble, but a deep laugh burst from him as he held Harey, the lad's legs clasping his waist and arms round his neck.

"Hell's blood, lad, Vina could do better than you." Gareth poked him in the ribs. "You need to stop slipping the game Maura sneaks into the stew to Owen and Vina if you want to knock my arse down." Harey squirmed, giggling as Gareth tickled him.

Maura closed in, her grin wide. "First to reach the creek gets to eat the egg Harey...borrowed from Argo this morn. Count of three. One...." She bolted past the pair, working her limbs as fast as she could. Someday, she would learn to stop flailing her arms.

A sharp whistle from Harey behind her, and Maura pushed even faster. The deep bay reached her ears, meaning Arturo was not dozing on the bed. Bitty would be hopping after the beast who no longer obeyed Gareth. Did Harey think a mere wolfhound could take her down? She would show who ruled this patch of Briton, if only she could gather air into her lungs—almost to the trees.

A heavy hand seized her elbow. She came to a dead halt, pitching forward.

Gareth scooped her up before she fell on her nose. Deep blue eyes sparkled down at her, while soft brown eyes watched from higher above. From his perch on Gareth's shoulders, Harey snickered and tugged on thick blond braids like reins. He clicked his tongue against his teeth, bumping his chin on Gareth's head and avoiding any contact with Maura crushed into the man's chest.

"A big man cannot lose to a wee lass who cheats," Gareth grumbled and stomped forward. "And the bloody lad raised by bloody hares can out-run a bloody dragon. How fair is that?" He stumbled around trees, angling for the deepest section of the creek.

"Dragon?" Harey squeaked. Arturo galloped past them, after the hare who had taken the lead.

"Maura will tell..." Gareth gasped, "when she's

done swearing." He winked at her.

The bubbling sounds of a rain-swollen creek reached her ears, along with the splash of Arturo leaping in. They cleared the trees. The sight of the waterfall cascading over the mound of rocks Gareth and Patrick had piled to create a deep pool, warned her of imminent danger. She opened her mouth to protest—too late. Powerful muscles tensed, and her body took flight.

She went down, sputtering. *Coldcoldcold.*

It took all her strength to break the surface. Knocking water from her ears, her feet paddling, she caught Harey's delighted whoop as Gareth flung him high.

Bastard threw the lad right beside her, and the wave knocked her under again. The waterlogged tunic dragged her down, and she struggled to reverse direction. No luck. Lungs burning, she closed her sight to the dappled afternoon sun slipping away.

Thank the gods, an arm—much too small for Gareth—wrapped around her waist. Her joyous exhale bubbled what little air she had left into the water.

Oh sweet lad, Harey has never touched me before.

Her head crested the surface and she gulped, chest heaving. She blinked her surprise as Harey's reedy legs kicked beneath his own billowing tunic, and he pulled and then heaved her onto the flat rocks beside the waterfall.

Droplets sprayed from her face as she shook her head. "Thank you, kind sir." She sat, drew her arms around her chest to hide tightened nipples, and smiled.

A shy duck of his head and Harey was off. He shot under, swimming like a dark eel directly back for Gareth watching from the bank.

"I see you, laddie," he yelled over the murmuring waterfall. He leaped, drew up and tucked his knees together, and crashed down on the ripples created by a lean lad.

A moment later, Harey headed toward the clouds in his grip. He bellowed with laughter as Gareth threw him behind him and then swam toward her.

His deep blue eyes glowed with happiness as Gareth jumped onto her rock. Water dripped, rainbow splatters onto the hard stone, surely reluctant to leave his lovely body. The tunic showed every firm line of his muscles, including the ridged cast of his cock as he collapsed beside her.

"Dragons, lass. Tell us about King Gareth who slew a winged beast eighteen feet long." He flung his arm around her, drawing her to his side.

Harey's turn to scamper onto the rocks. He shook water from his face, most likely an attempt to hide his flush as he bypassed her to take Gareth's other side.

"That cannot be right." He leaned onto Gareth's chest to smile, shy and sweet, at her. He inched as close as flesh would allow. "Is not the king named Harey, and the runt the size of a chicken who cleans the horse droppings called Gareth the Slow? Can a dragon fly faster than a falcon? Are they real? Where...?"

His yelp was cut off as Gareth slapped his hand over his mouth. Gareth pulled free of Maura, seized Harey and this time he got thrown almost clear across the thirty foot span of water.

Gareth dropped and gathered her under his arm. They watched Harey bounding from the water headed for the hound sniffing at something by the pines, Bitty dry and safe beside him.

"Did you remember about Arturo?" Gareth murmured.

"Yes, dear heart," she said. Heat filled her belly as his large hand nudged beneath her breasts. "Each day until the snow is too high in the fields, Harey slaves at the dark castle. The brave prince does chores and weeps into the pillow of his knight on a fool's quest. He lies on your bed, learns to read falsehoods, uses precious ink to form thoughts onto parchment about a god who fears women and bastards."

"Precisely. Except for the weeping, but—"

"Arturo never leaves his side. The mighty wolfhound will rip out the throat of any lord who attempts to defile a virgin." Maura jerked her chin up to peek at her lover. "I fear he is going to follow you. How can I stop that? He will not abide my touch, let alone my words."

"Good. Only I get your touch. Soon, dear gods, soon or my cock will burst and not in a good way."

"Forget your bloody cock. What will happen come sunrise?"

"I commanded a village to prepare for war against one lad. Broch, Argo, Colin and Derick will pretend to escort me to the abbey. In reality, I will be under guard so I cannot follow my heart's desire and double back to stay the winter in the bed of the most beautiful maid to walk this earth."

She blinked back her tears. "How does that keep Harey, who's only three years younger than you, from following his heart's desire?"

"Eighty-six men, forty women, and thirty-some children will hang if they do not catch hold of him."

Maura sighed. "Impossible. No number of humans can hold the wind."

"I know. Vina is hiding Bitty. He will never be like your da, Maura. He will not abandon you, Vina, and especially the blasted hare. Not even for me."

A moment later, a small form streaked across the pool. Gareth opened his other arm, and Harey curled into the comfort.

"Dragons?" he mumbled.

"The year of our lord 495, in some distant land named Denmark, a mighty chieftain—Beowulf—was birthed. Fifty-some years later, a fearsome winged monster removed his head. The beast choked on king's blood and stopped eating the charred flesh of man. Thank the gods, a tall and strong warrior greater than any mere wolf—Harey the Swift—learned of the fire-breathing beast roasting hares across Briton."

As he babbled to a spellbound Harey, Maura felt her eyelids closing.

ଔ

A thrill ran from her chest down into her stomach. Strong fingers worked at her nipple, hardening it into a firm bud. A large hand cupped her breast? *Oh, oh, oh.* "Gareth?" she gasped.

The press of a thick cock prodded her completely awake.

She smacked hand and arm aside and sat up. On the rocks, beside the pool.

Naked as the day he was born, Gareth shot his hand under her dried tunic. She slapped him. "Stop."

"Cannot. I will die. Help me." He blotted out the sun hanging low in the sky, reaching his mouth for hers.

"Harey—"

"Making a feast." He murmured the words against her mouth. "Worried Vina would return from Owen's to an empty home." He took her lips, his tongue jabbing in and out of her delighted mouth, perfect rhythm with the hand rubbing her exposed thigh, angling closer and closer for the moisture gathering between her legs.

She began returning his kiss with the desperation of a woman facing a five to six month drought.

Chapter Five

Vernal Equinox AD 613

One foot slapped the ground and then the other. Sweat trickled down Harey's face, and his heart felt as if it would burst with sorrow. It had been a wonderful year since he and Bitty had found happiness, but he had thrown it all away. He had let greed ruin him, and eaten too many pilfered eggs. Along with the delicious yellow yolk, bright as the sun, dark evil had also filled his belly. It would not have been a problem if the wickedness had not spread even lower as well.

He had waited for this special day, when the night would last as long as the day, for months now with joy—and for forty-five long days and nights, with dread. He ran, fast as he could, toward the best and the worst thing that could happen on a cool spring afternoon. Any second, around the very next bend, he would see the grey mare and a man with dark blue eyes holding the reins.

It seemed like ten thousand years since Gareth had visited last. Harey hated the monastery of Bangor with its harsh, angry god. He loved how Gareth talked on and on about ancient scrolls and foreign lands with happy light in his eyes. But when he jabbered about angels and demons and life after death, Harey yearned to throw his arms around him and beg him to worry about the here and now.

Fear rose from his flying toes, through his body and out his ears. It—the here and now—was no longer his concern. Fate marked him. He was a bad man, just like his da had been and there was nothing he could do to change that. Because he had failed to be good—twenty-eight times—this bright day was to be his last. But no matter how twisted his heart felt, or how many tears fought to leap from his eyes, hot glee filled him. *Gareth. I get to hug him—before he kills me.*

Harey skidded to a halt. Bit, her six kittens, and one greyhound bumped into his ankles and leg. He ignored them and flexed his arm. Maybe, just maybe, he could take Gareth down before he placed his hands around Harey's neck and squeezed. Pampered by everyone, stuffed with the best foods, he had grown very strong.

Arturo perked his ears. A low growl from the dog, and he perked his own ears. He charged forward and pumped his knees so hard he consistently lost contact with the ground.

There.

His heart swelled. He ran even faster. Gareth's smile lit Harey's blood, and it felt like every nerve within him came to a boil. The most beautiful man in the world slowed the mare and hopped off.

At the sight of Gareth's arms opening wide, he became coiled tighter than ever before. He sprang into flight in a tremendous leap. His body stretched out, he drew his legs apart and struck a broad chest.

Gareth laughed, stumbled, and wrapped his arms

around him. He regained his balance and held tight with Harey's legs clamped around his waist. Harey snuggled his face under Gareth's chin and gulped deep breaths of the wondrous musk and ink and leather scent that was his Gareth.

"Greetings. Gods, you run fast. Catch your breath. I missed you, too, my lad."

Harey's heart plunged to his toes. He sucked in air and drew back to scowl. "No. Can you not tell? Feel how hard I hit you? I am no longer a lad, Gareth; I am a man. I really missed you. I worry that I am dreaming. Put me down. Let me jump on you again. I can knock you flat. I know I can."

Gareth had tightened, stiff as a dead hare. Something was wrong. Either he could feel the shame twisting and burning within Harey, or he regretted his arms around a man? "Sorry? You do not want me to be a man?"

"Of course I do, but why such a hurry to grow up?" Gareth settled him on his feet and shrugged free of his arms. "Let me see you. Amazing. You are six inches taller, and you have added some weight, but you barely reach my chin. The day you jump like a crazed hare on me and do knock me over is the day I dread. Yet nothing for you to fret about."

Dying was nothing to worry about? Gareth did not care? He must understand how evil Harey was. He must be able to tell just by looking that he was no longer special. Self-loathing slammed into him. He had lost Gareth's affection, and now he could not wait to die. His very own spring festival on this day, cold blue eyes the last thing he would see.

"I am sorry, but you are wrong. I'm a man now—and not a good one." Harey fisted his tunic and swallowed his dread. "There is something I have to tell you. Will you walk with me?"

"Of course, lad...er, man. But explain what has happened first." Gareth stopped stroking Arturo and looked up. He smiled and warmth burst into Harey. Until he remembered his multitude of sin, and the jitters filled his stomach.

Gareth tousled his hair. "Cannot be all that bad. Did you steal so many eggs from Argo, he has had a stroke? Break Maura's heart because you are still sleeping outside when I am gone? Feed all the radishes and carrots Vina grew to the hares?"

*Confess, confess, confess...*Harey swallowed hard. "Iamnotavirginsorry."

"Excuse me?"

"I am no longer a virgin. Please do not hate me." Harey looked up, and loosened all his fear from his heart.

Deep blue eyes flashed storm grey. His lips tight, fists knotted at his sides, Gareth heaved a sharp exhale. "I will kill whoever laid a hand on you. Argo? My brother? Who touched you?"

Tell him. Just tell him. Eyes on the ground, Harey blurted his guilt. "I did. I touched me. Goodness squirted out. White and sticky. And then, I did it again and again. I am sorry that I disappointed you. Owen promises to care for Bitty and her brood. Arturo will see them back to Owen. Too evil for the festival under the moon, so can I die in the sun? You will kill me, not your brother? Please?"

The air frozen in his lungs, he waited for strong fingers to snap his neck. He did not expect the howl that sprung from Gareth's lips. So much laughter, Gareth bent like he had broken something inside of him.

Harey found his fingers curling into fists. Brows knotted, he snapped, "Cannot you just sacrifice me already, must you mock me first?"

"S-sorry! I am so sorry." Gareth straightened and his chortle turned soft with affection. He wrapped his arms around Harey. "Yes. You are certainly a man now. But get one thing straight, sweetheart. No one is going to kill you. You have done nothing wrong. I rub my cock quite often, ever since I was much younger than you. Because you have had a solid year of proper nourishment, you have matured. It is a man's thing, and it is not wrong. I should have guessed. Your voice has dropped. You grew a lot of hair down there now, yes?"

I am not evil? Really? He could not believe his ears.

Gareth patted his back. "Shh. You are good and sweet and everything is fine. Now, about that hair?"

"Yes. Gareth? Being a virgin does not matter? You do not hate me?"

Gareth squeezed him so tightly, he feared his heart would leap from his chest with happiness. He held his breath.

"Hate you? Never. I should have explained things to you sooner." Gareth drew back. "Unless you pushed between a woman's legs and fucked her, you are considered pure. Er...men can do that to other men. In the arse. It is not right with someone unwilling or naive as you, and I worried a bastard would have at you if I did not tell everyone to leave you be. Do you understand?"

"Oh. Yes. No. If Maura's bathing, and Vina or Owen are wrestling on top of me, and most of all, if I think about missing you, well, it is all right?"

Gareth's Adam's apple bobbed deep. "Yes. Keep it private, though. Some think it to be...doesn't make sense, the beliefs. Just make sure you are always alone. Remember the salve I used on your leg and scars last year?"

He nodded. Joy filled him. Not only was this another wondrous day of life, the color flushing Gareth's face would be a sweet memory to rub to. Soon as possible.

"It will ease any rough spots." He glanced at Harey worming his fingers into his hand. "You know, you can ask Patrick things if I am not around. How long have you been worried about this?" He squeezed Harey's hand and reached to gather up the reins.

"Not long," Harey lied. "When will I be big enough...to be a man for Eostre?"

The smile fled Gareth's lips. "I promise I will explain all this spring sacrifice nonsense, when you are as tall as me. Most important, know I love you and will never let anything bad happen to you. Now, tell me about Maura. Did that sod Colin get her to kiss him? Share her bed?"

He shook his head. "I do not like him. I sleep with Maura when he is not hunting or slaughtering men who try and take this land."

Gareth halted and pretended to snarl. "What? Did I hear right? You are the man a stupid arse of a monk needs to worry about?"

Harey grinned. "Yes. If you do not cease living with all those men and tell your cruel brother to let you stay with me, next time you come home mayhap Maura will have a litter of mine. Between her legs, you said?"

Gareth's laugh filled Harey's heart. Hand in hand they strolled. Gareth told him things he had learned from dusty manuscripts this past year. Every detail, except how Harey could make the angel he loved stay with him instead of God.

Chapter Six

Sprawled on the hard straw, Gareth lay awake and knew the man beside him did the same. It had been three years since an abused orphan had reached puberty. Gareth had not expected the rush, intensity of feeling this afternoon when Harey grabbed onto him for the first time in six months—and stood eye to eye with him. The only remnants of the runt he had carried away from the high waterfall were the scars on Harey's backside.

Eighteen, he still could not knock Gareth down, but his bones ached after the attempts. Harey certainly had tried, and Gareth had to make a dangerous decision soon, before he lost the pair he loved.

Soft, dainty snores came from his other side. Under the rising moon, he had fucked Maura hard and fast against a tree. Then flat on the ground, slow and sensual, he had licked and tongued her moist, sweet spot until she had climaxed against his mouth. He cleaned his seed off her stomach with his tunic, and she had wept years of frustration against his shoulder.

He had asked Patrick to distract Harey, and hoped the lad—Gareth smiled as he corrected his thoughts—the young man had not followed and watched from the shadows. It was all Gareth could do not to grab Harey and see what kissing a man—*arsehole*—a man had awaited him this special day, yes, but not emotionally matured.

Sweet and naïve as a bairn, he was unlike any other in existence, thanks to his tragic upbringing. With an unfettered imagination, a mind more inquisitive and brilliant than all the esteemed scholars at the abbey put together, Harey's eyes flamed with love-lust whenever he thought Gareth was not looking. Such purity of soul, untainted innocence, Gareth's legs wobbled as he snuck peeks right back.

Harey knew what Gareth had doomed him for, and he still idolized him with all his huge heart. How could Gareth take advantage of that? How could he sleep in the middle, knowing he yearned for a man, a woman, and a celibate life at the abbey?

Maura, I love you. Gareth thought of her soft lips, her stomach empty of his child, during every moment he was parted from her.

Harey, I love you. Tall and lean, he ran faster than the wind, but no one could outrun an arrow drawn from behind a tree. Whenever those wide brown eyes flashed into Gareth's mind, he imagined all sorts of nasty things. When he remembered Harey's fingers working into his, he grew hard and hungry and fell to his knees, and rubbed and rubbed.

Books, ink, solitude, I love you. So what? He would give it up in a heartbeat. He would till the fields, work as a serf with joy in his heart, and Maura would be his every night, if not for his bastard of a brother. Broch had made it clear. If Gareth refused to take vows, pray for the soul of an arse constantly, he would come home to find Harey hanging from a tree and Maura bedded with Colin Bratton.

It looked like Gareth would be in for a long night, but he would have many hours to rest alone. Right now, as soft female curves pressed against one side and hard male flesh against the other, he did not dare sleep. God knew what he might do in his dreams.

"Gareth?"

The soft whisper filled his ear. "Yes, Harey, I am awake."

"May I show you something? Down past the creek?"

"Yes. I will wake Maura."

Harey's breath caught, his body stiffened. Gareth rolled, pushing him from the mattress. "Oh? No lasses then. Men only."

His relieved sigh went straight to Gareth's heart. They tiptoed out the door. He swallowed the lump in his throat as Harey grasped his hand and pulled him for the trees.

The cold breeze, silver glow of the full moon, crisp scent of pine—the night belonged to the goddess and lust raged in plant, animal, and man as spring shoved winter aside.

"Harey, where are we going?"

He yanked his hand loose and smacked Gareth's lips. "Stay quiet and follow." He caressed his fingers over Gareth's chin and dropped his hand.

Gareth swallowed a mountain of lust, dipped his head and bowed him onward. Twists and turns, a half mile later he parted a low branch and tugged Gareth to break free of the trees.

They fell into a squat and Harey flipped his fingers toward the clearing.

Gareth's breath caught. Under the glimmering lunar orb, twenty to thirty hares chased each other in a riotous display of energy, in circles and dashes throughout the soft, low meadow grasses. Couples sprang up to dance, boxing their front paws against each other. Tapping and hitting and smacking, until one stayed low and scampered as the other pursued.

Harey's low chuckle brushed his ear. "Breathe," he whispered and inched his thigh closer. "Silly, are they not?"

Gareth drew in a deep breath. He had never seen anything like it. Drunk on life and moonlight, they looked like they were having such fun and paid no attention to the lurking humans.

He turned to Harey's bright eyes and whispered, "Sweet lord—they do this all the time? A mating competition?"

Harey shook his head. "They mate year round. Most are already paired. But it is a fine night, under this moon. The snow melts. The ground thaws. Carrots will soon grow. They are happy."

Gareth did not know what was more breathtaking, the moonlight glimmering in Harey's soft eyes, or the rowdy dance. "Are any of these Bitty's offspring?"

Harey grinned and pointed. "That couple rolling over there is her daughter with the buck she chose last spring. The one chasing to the left is Bit's fat son from three litters ago who tries to mate his brother's choice and gets clobbered. And...."

The man beside him stiffened. Gareth turned.

A huge bob of Harey's Adam's apple and he gestured again. "The biggest two in the center hitting each other, one is a buck who turned up last summer. He is...interested in Sam."

Gareth swallowed hard. "Sam?"

Harey dropped his gaze. "Yes. I have seen every kit Bitty has birthed, and Samuel is the largest. He might not be ready to mate for more than this dance. He is only seven months old, but so big he wants to play—and fuck. The hares, they do not care if it is evil and no kittens will grow."

The air slammed from his lungs. *Oh sweet God. What amazing things happened under this moon?* He pushed the words straight from his heart and past his lips. "Not evil. It is beautiful."

Harey spun, his eyes huge. "Really? I think so, too. Gareth? Can...we...." His voice cracked and he jerked his sight back on the hares.

Gareth fought his aching cock. "No. Ask me again when you are taller than me. Oh, look over there. Three...play together?"

Harey turned to the meadow's edge. "I do not know. I have only seen two hit at each other before. Er...Gareth? I have never noticed bucks pair until this big one came around. You sure it is not wrong? That is—" His jaw dropped. He slapped himself in the forehead. "I am sorry. I forgot. I would no longer be a virgin. I understand. Did I say sorry?"

Every hare huddled down as Harey jumped to his feet, his voice no longer a whisper. "I need to leave."

Gareth did not stand a chance of catching him. He was already gone into the trees as Gareth found his tongue. "Damn it, Harey. Stop." The hares scattered while he scrambled to run. "You had best obey me!" He thrashed into the forest and ran smack into a rigid chest.

Hard to see in the moonlight filtered by foliage, but he could feel the streaks of moisture on Harey's face. He pulled him into his arms. "You should remain a virgin so my pagan brother does not hang you." *Arsehole that I am, I want you for myself. Soon as I figure things out.* "Broch knows everything happening in his territory, including who dances with whom. Wait for me to deal with this. I will not let any heathens kill you, Harey. I promise."

He snorted. "You will not be here. You would rather stay with those monks than me. You would fuck a man of God, Gareth? I am not good enough for you?"

Gareth jerked his face up, slammed his rigid cock against him, and brushed his mouth with his lips. He thrust Harey from him and stepped back. "Not now. Maybe never. Not even when you are stronger or taller than me. You are not mature yet. You only try to please me, are not thinking of your own needs, and most of all there is Maura. I have been a sod to her, but at least I have been faithful."

The sight of wounded brown eyes seared into his heart, and Gareth angled to do what he did best. Flee. "I need more time. But know that I have not been, nor ever will be, with any man but you."

Gareth ran. No way could he outpace an upset youth raised by hares, but his stomach clenched. The sound of Harey coming to overtake him failed to reach his ears.

Nor did he see the lad grown to a man as he kissed Maura farewell and began his long journey back.

෫

Gareth held the reins slack in his hands and felt like he had fought his gloom for an eternity. The loud crack of a branch disturbed his brooding and he jerked. He had left his heart a four hour ride behind him, but it suddenly returned to fill his chest and tried to leap out of his mouth. Whatever had been following him, wanted its presence known. He halted the mare and scanned the forest edge.

Harey jumped from the trees and trudged to his side.

Gareth was off the mare and on his feet in a beat of

a fevered heart. "Oh God, sweetheart. I cannot believe you have run this far. Here, let me hold you. Breathe." Gareth wrapped his arms around him.

Soon as his chest stopped heaving, Gareth pushed him back. A finger under Harey's chin raised his face. "Where's Arturo? Bit's not with you?"

Harey tried to smile. "Tired from dancing, she did not stir. I snuck past the greyhound with ease, as well."

"Maura?"

"I am not running away. I will go back. The bairns, they look up to me. Maura needs me to keep Colin away. I hit him, you know. Two months past. I *am* a *mature* man, despite what you think."

Gareth swallowed hard. "You attacked Colin?"

Harey snorted. "He told Brochfael the Tarse he fell in the woods. It embarrassed him that Eostre's little hare could blacken his face." He yanked open a flap on his tunic and pulled out a folded thick parchment. He shoved it at Gareth. "Here. I am sorry. I will pray every day to gods I hate for your safe return. Farewell."

"Harey, wait!"

He skidded to a halt. Ran back. Flung his arms round Gareth and hugged him. As Gareth leaned, homing in on his mouth, he pulled free.

One blink and he had disappeared into the trees.

Gareth sighed. He opened the booklet. Perfect Latin, the letters precise and painstakingly drawn to conserve parchment, it looked like a journal. Harey had given him a priceless gift, moments with Maura and Vina that he had shared and Gareth had not.

His soul weary, he climbed back on the mare. He had taught Harey letters, numbers, all he knew of the world. In return, he showed him that no fabricated sacrifice to a pagan goddess was worth this much heartache.

He would not risk waiting much longer. Best to flee

before the snows hit. This fall, he would raid Broch's stables, take four horses, two sisters, and start a new life far from here with Harey by his side.

CS

Time dragged by, his backside almost as sore as his heart before Gareth clucked the mare down the steep slope, and readied to begin the sharp ascent along the dark pathway into Bangor. He had spent the past hour wishing he, and all those he loved, lived in a day and age when religions did not matter. That all men cared about was the present, and how they behaved in each moment for the sake of the moment, not the fear of eternal damnation or hopes for bounteous reward in an afterlife.

Perhaps if he could spend the mornings dreaming with Jonathon and Niall. Instead of praying in silence to a quiet God, they might come up with a revolutionary means to ease the isolation. Jonathon's latest idea filled Gareth's head. Imagine a way to message safer and faster than use of man, bird, or fires. A means to converse other than ink and quill onto dried animal skins, expensive parchment delivered on horseback or attached to the leg of a vulnerable pigeon, and doomed to arrive haphazardly days or months later, into the hands of the elite few able to read.

Jonathon had rambled about using sound. Clicks and clacks, a code translating into words, flung into the air as far as possible, captured and then sent out again and again until they reached the ears of a loved one. How sweet would it be to talk to Harey and Maura as if miles did not separate them?

It would be almost as sweet as losing those bloody miles once and for all. Gareth's resolve hardened. No matter the fear locking its claws into his guts, he must not risk jeopardizing Maura, Vina, and a naïve Harey who would not be able to spear a rat, let alone a man.

Outside of Brochfael's keep, those he loved would rely on him for protection, and he would see his life's blood spill before harm fell to them. The moment the first snowflake fluttered to the ground, when his tarse of a brother would least expect it, Gareth aimed to slink away from his studies and abandon the monastery.

He would give reason for mighty Lord Brochfael, a patriarchal god, and a lusty goddess to damn him to become a fallen angel's bitch in hell, and he would do it with a song of joy in his heart.

A powerful trio to fight against, but his mind, heart, soul, and *cock* could not face another winter without the pair he missed more than hope of salvation lying on either side of him.

Of course, running for the seaside and sailing far from the isle of Briton did not solve the dilemma of Maura. Surely she knew Gareth's darkest secret. That each time he jumped her, worked in and out of her with a cock harder than the staff of Moses, her loving green eyes blurred into a man's muddy brown. Her smooth cheeks grew stubble, and soft breasts disappeared into the bony ribs of a thin, tall man who could run faster than this bloody mare. A man who asked him for his kiss and more, and he—*I hate myself*—had said no.

Gareth needed the privacy of his room, his salve, and his hand.

Beneath the dim moonlight, he urged the weary mare into a trot along the narrow dirt path, under the arch, and up the slope to the rear entrance of the vast sleeping quarters where well over a thousand men lay slumbering.

"Gareth?" A low voice called out, jarring him into

full alert.

The hooded figure stepped into view and Gareth yanked the mare to a halt. He settled back into his skin and stared down at the monk throwing off his cowl to expose his face in the moonlight.

"Greetings, Cynric." He slid his sore body off the mare. *Why the hell is this arse awake?*

Cynric reached for the reins. "Long ride, Gareth. Glad you have finally returned. I have missed you." He started to tug the mare for the stables. "Let me tend to her for you." The monk hurried off before he gathered his wits to protest.

He slumped and headed in the opposite direction, entered under the sweeping granite archway, climbed the steps, and walked down the silent corridors, past closed door after closed door, twisting and bearing south until he reached his own.

One thing about having a powerful lord for a brother, Gareth did not have to share quarters. Cynric hailed from upper Brittany. He too could have a private room, but the man who had taken his vows already, a monk only a year older than Gareth, did not care for solitary rest.

Last spring, a student—Eadmar—pleaded for audience with the stern monk in charge of housing. The request for a different roommate had been denied. Two days later, a rough bruise on his face found the lad on the other side of the abbey, and Cynric alone with his guilt. Gareth did not care to hear what the larger man claimed in confessional. Eadmar's flinch was enough for him to ready his fists whenever he witnessed the pair cross paths.

Eostre and Christ only knew how long Cynric had stood in the shadows, waiting for his return.

The weight of the long summer nights ahead tumbled down upon him as he entered his dusty, dark room and fumbled for the chair in the corner. He propped it under the doorknob. He stripped off his tunic, pulled down and kicked free of his pants, and ran his fingers through his hair as he took the five steps to his bed.

It was not until he landed on top of a naked man, felt rough fingers slap over his mouth and a knee in his side flipping them both off the straw to the stone, Gareth flat on his back, did the howl escape his throat.

"Shhh," whispered the bastard lying over him. "I will not harm you. It is me, Gareth. Me." The hand fell from his mouth.

"Fucking tarse," Gareth snapped. "I know 'tis you, Cynric. Get off me before I wake everyone here."

"No. Please." His head shot down, his lips took Gareth's, and the man ground his hard cock against Gareth's stomach.

His lips pressed tight, he reacted without thought or care that his own cock had perked up with interest. He jerked his arm loose and jammed his fist into Cynric's kidney.

Cynric gasped, and Gareth's fingers jabbing into his throat took the man's mouth off his.

"Please." Cynric groaned. "I love you."

Love? The look on Harey's thin face, the adoration and longing whenever he thought Gareth would not notice, had haunted him for three years. The memory of the hopelessness filling those wounded brown eyes when Gareth had said no to his cock pressing into Gareth just like this bastard's did now, sent anger snarling through his veins. He had no need to pretend sincerity in the quiet words falling from his lips. "Move, or you are a dead man."

Cynric rolled aside.

Praise the goddess, darkness hid the man's cock, and based on the strangled sound, his tears as well.

Gareth shoved himself to his feet and shifted to sit on the bed. Thank the Christ, his own cock had deflated. It now hung as limp as moldy straw. "Stop sniveling. Where is my horse?"

"I had Marden..." Cynric's low voice cracked with a sob, "ready to take her."

Gareth drew his hand across his lips, rubbing the feel of Cynric away. The man had raced around, entered through the front, and jumped into his bed before he reached the room.

Cynric stirred and Gareth snapped, "Stay down. You cannot force me like the little lad Eadmar."

"I care not. Kill me. Please."

He snorted. "What in the name of Christ is wrong with you?"

"I-I am so lonely. It has been two years, almost to the day, since my...lover...." Cynric drew a shuddering breath and quieted.

Gareth broke the silence. "Something happened to...him?" Although the lasses would love his deep green eyes, strong clean looks, and sturdy build, Gareth could not imagine him crying over a woman.

"Dead. My da claimed him a horse thief. Said I am an abomination to God. Made me come here."

Gareth heaved a sigh. "You have my compassion. But your misfortunate is no excuse. You really think you could rape me? I am no skinny little lad."

Cynric sat up. "I did not...yes, I did. I am sick. Evil. And I miss the only man who ever thought otherwise. I should be burning in hell with him."

"Had he taken a horse?"

For a long moment, Cynric did not answer. "I stole two. Three nights in the woods were the happiest of my life. We made it to the seaside before my da and brothers caught up. Da said one of us had to accept responsibility. My lover begged for my life and I said nothing. I do not deserve to live.".

Gareth rubbed the exhaustion from his eyes. "Maybe not, but that should be left to fate. If you would stop being a tarse, seek forgiveness from Eadmar, make sure the fear stays out of his eyes every time he sees you, you would find some peace. If your da really thought you an abomination, he would have hung the both of you instead of giving you to God and twelve hundred men, one of whom might enjoy you on top of him."

"I wanted you. I know...I hear you talking about this Harey. Is he why you will not have me?"

Gareth sighed. He reached for the monk's robe he could feel wadded against the wall and flung it to Cynric. "Throw me my tunic, then stay down, or I swear you will get your wish to join your lover."

As soon as Gareth pulled the tunic on, whacked his complaining cock that throbbed the moment Harey's face filled his mind into submission, he sighed again. "Harey and I—that is complicated. Yes, I love him. More than life, deities, brother, or any bastard monk who wants to fuck me and never will. He is so sweet, beautiful, and completely daft over me."

"Then you have had him," Cynric muttered. "Over and over and you want only him. That is why you can never care for a sinner like me."

"No," he snapped. He flung himself down on his back. "I have never been with a man before and you do not know Harey. He is...not normal. I sometimes think he is not entirely human. Abused since birth, I found him when he was fifteen, and I marked him in a deceitful way for my own. Once he reached manhood, that is. But he is a bloody saint, and I am afraid he would do anything to please me, just to please me, and if I ever hurt him I will roll over for Lucifer alongside you."

His cock jerked again, hardening against his thigh

as Maura's face, sparkling green eyes, the sweet circle of her mouth softly open in arousal, rippled through his thoughts. "And there is this lass involved. Five wonderful years."

A sharp laugh grunted from Cynric. "You have a lad *and* a lass in love with you, while I cannot even get a kiss? You asked what is wrong with me. I wish I knew."

Gareth smiled to himself, and pretended a man sprawled on his left, a woman curled on his right, and a hare pressed against his toes. "I am no expert, but I think if you could treat a lad like you would a lass. Bring him the softest crust of fresh bread, a handful of flowers, and if he says no, accept it and move on. One of these men might just smile. Maura did. Her smile filled my heart for months, before I dared even kiss her. I would never jump her in the dark. I split wood, brought game, waited for her to come of age along with me, and had to abandon them both for God."

At least my loves still walk the earth. Cynric's confidence concerning his path to the abbey pierced Gareth's heart. A man murders, rapes, beats his wife and bairn, and their lord could pardon. Take a loaf of bread or a horse; it ends with rope round a neck.

For how long will one of my loves walk this earth? Thanks to his idiotic encouragement, Harey would have poached hundreds of eggs from Argos by now. Enough to have the life choked from him a thousand times over. Bitterness filled his heart. The lad destined for blood spilt under the fat spring moon might not dangle from a tree in the near future. Instead, his neck could be snapped by his asinine brother in a fit of rage. The sooner Gareth took his loves and ran the better.

He sighed as he heard Cynric collapse backward against the stone floor. "Why have you not brought at least this Harey here?"

Gareth stiffened. "Brought him here?"

"Even if the woman has some claim on you, you could arrange him to be taken on as a student. Let him warm the bed you have made with God, and have her in your bed at home. Mathew has done that and Stephen, as well. My arsehole da made sure I never want to see him or anyone in my family again. With someone...like you, I would happily pray my life away for my da, hate the pagans, and give praise to the Christ with every breath."

Gareth curled his fingers into a fist as he heard Cynric shove to his feet. He stared up at the man peering down at him.

"Please forgive me. I am—"

"Off to your own room? An hour of sleep before prayers, avoid the fat monk who likes to slap arses while we scrub pots in the kitchen, and join Jonathon, Niall, and me in the gardens—right, my friend?"

Sounded like Cynric swallowed a sob. "Yes...my friend. Good night."

As soon as Gareth heard him quietly set aside the chair, open and close the door behind him, his body relaxed while his mind whirled. A few miles from the abbey, a home could shelter a lass and her little sister. Might Harey find happiness in the arms of a woman in the nearby village? The life of a man who preferred other men could end with both hanging from a tree, thieves or not.

Selfish tarse that he was, if he pushed Harey to lose any remaining fear of women resulting from his tragic childhood, he would have a chance for happiness far from Brochfael's keep. The plan failed, there was always murder to contemplate.

No matter Gareth was the devil who fated Harey to have his blood drained in a pagan ceremony, he would slit his elder brother's throat before harm could come to Eostre's hare.

Chapter Seven

In the year of our Lord, AD 616

*M*aura washed the dust from her table and sighed. It had been two months since Gareth and Harey had some sort of fight, and Gareth returned to his books. She did her best to cheer Harey, but he had moped for days and spent hours running in the woods.

Thankfully this summer morn, she had the means to distract a lovesick man. Yes, there was no doubt in her mind that Harey remained innocent and sweet as a babe, but he simmered with a man's lust and anger deep within him.

She turned to the doorway and rolled her eyes at the lad skipping toward her. "I said yellow flowers, Owen, not blue. We already have blue stain. Where is our Har?"

Owen grinned. He pulled a handful of buttercups from behind his back and tossed them to join the others on the table. "I picked the bluebells for you and Vina. I shall marry that lass, did I tell you that before?"

Maura smiled. "Yes, dear, you mention it every

day." Her smile widened for the man trailing behind him. Right on mark, the jitters in her stomach burst into a frenzy. Tall, lean, and virile, Harey had grown into an attractive man, and as she gazed up into soft mud-colored eyes, she yearned to do many bad things. "Greetings, Harey. You see what Owen found?"

He nodded. "Lovely. The color will bring big smiles from the little ones." He patted himself, pulled six eggs from his pockets, and set them carefully on the table. He tucked two newly born leverets back into his tunic and turned to go. "The lads, lasses are always hungry. I will check under the hens again. If you try and follow me, O-lad, I will tie you to a tree. That arse Argo almost caught you."

"Harey! Do not use such language." Maura slumped. She did not know why she bothered. No one listened to her fussing.

"Why the tarse, arse, sod, not?" Owen chimed. "Yell at me, not him. I taught him. Harey, stay. Let us boil those eggs. I cannot wait to see if yellow flowers are prettier than blue ink. I tell you though. Red is the way to go."

Maura groaned at Owen. "You are not dying eggs bloody red. Pink, maybe, and it will be your blood we use to stain them."

"Not now, O-lad," Harey said. "My regrets, but there are bairns waiting for me to fatten them up before the druids or the Romans slit their throats."

"Harey, sit down," Maura snapped. "Owen, leave."

Owen dropped to the floor. Harey sighed and stared at his feet.

"Owen—I said go home."

The brat hugged his knees, stuck his tongue out, and left his arse in place. "Harey's my friend and I stand...sit by him."

"Oh for the love of Eostre who does not want blood

sacrifice and never did. Stay quiet then." Maura turned to Harey. "Boil water. Colleen's been sickly, right? She will love a bright yellow egg."

"Yes. And Danny, Brit, and Jose did not get a blue one last week. Argo has finally learned to count past three." Harey raised his bitter gaze to Maura. "I should take those hens from him. They need more area to peck in. The hounds and most of all, fat Argo, frightens them. And why does the stupid man think a cock is needed? The hens would lay more if he would leave them be. Doesn't matter how many times the cock mounts them. When chicks are happy, the eggs fall fertile or not."

She swallowed hard. "I beg you not to confront him. We—none of us—can bear to lose you. Eggs matter naught if our beloved Har's harmed. Give me your word."

"I have told you before. I will not leave you. Not until Gareth comes home to stay." Harey mumbled so she could barely hear. "The sod. A good man would wed you and run me off."

"Kick the other rooster out?" Maura forced a grin. "Not Gareth. You know that." She joined Harey in a sigh. Gareth was selfish, no doubt. Try as he did to hide it, he lusted even more than she did. The man fled to his monastery to avoid his sins, leaving her in heat and angst for months. *Common harlot—that's me.* Yearning for two hard cocks on either side of her made her not only lustful, but greedy as well. No wonder she had been fated to lie alone almost year round.

She raised her sight from long toes, lean limbs, lingered on groin area, bony chest, thick braided hair...*stop it, you heathen wench.* "What happened between you and him?"

"Nothing. I just miss him. Sorry." His sullen brown eyes softened and Harey smiled. "You know how I like green things? I found a plant. I will roll a few leaves, light them on fire and puff the smoke while I rub some salve on my...er...legs. Then I shall go for a run and not be so grumpy. Thank you for another color. After I get back, I will sneak them to the lucky ones."

Owen hopped to his feet and Harey snapped his fingers. "O-lad, stay. I really must run fast." Starting forward, he froze. He angled his head to listen, and then spun back to the table. He scooped the eggs into the small kettle, and tucked it behind Maura's drying tunic.

"Harey?" She raised her brows.

"Horses." He strode across the floor and peered out the doorway. "Brochfael's in the lead. Argo and Colin follow. Stay inside."

Who the hell did these blasted men think she was? A useless scrap of linen to step on? A wench to cook and clean for them? *Yes, m'lord. No, m'lord. Up your arse, m'lord.* Maura was sick of Harey trying to shield her from Colin Bratton. Despite how lonely her bed was, no meant no. What could they want?

Her heartbeat stuttered. Had something happened to Gareth?

Maura hurried to Owen, smacked him aside, and stood beside Harey. Her courage raced off, screaming at the sight of Gareth's brother. The man looked furious.

Brochfael yanked hard on the black stallion, and froth spit from the poor creature's mouth as it slowed, stumbling and kicking up clumps of dirt.

"Harey?" Brochfael bellowed.

He pulled free from Maura's frantic grasp of his tunic and sprang into the path of the horse. Grabbing the reins, he trotted with the beast. Soothing clucks from Harey, the exhausted horse gained its balance and halted. He patted the animal, released the reins, and stared at Brochfael.

A hush fell, and then Brochfael's clipped words assaulted Maura's ears. "Aethelfrith, King of Northumbria, led fifty thousand Saxons into my territory at the Vale of Chester. Twelve hundred unarmed priests and students from the monastery of Bangor marched. They attempted to aid with their prayers. Massacred. Cut down by heathen blade—every last man."

Maura's heart cracked. Owen grabbed her elbow as the world tilted black.

"No." Harey's voice rang out. "Not every last man. He lives. I shall find him." He readied to run.

"Wait." Brochfael swung his leg around and dismounted. "Bangor burns. Halls, colleges, churches, and libraries, all in ruins. God has smote me and mine."

Argo and Colin came to a stop behind Brochfael. Harey did not acknowledge them. His grim gaze rested on Brochfael. "I say it again. I *will* find Gareth and pray you, our mighty lord find courage. Gareth worried there would be consequence, clash between pagan and Rome. You left them unprotected. How could you? Why are you not smiting the bastards who did this? Before they murder more innocents?"

"You little sodden lad. Don't—"

Brochfael signaled Argo to be quiet. "I depart within the hour and head for Dee. You will ride to Chester, locate my brother?"

Harey nodded.

"Argo, give him your horse," Brochfael said.

"I do not want a horse," Harey said. "I want help. Patrick and his eldest, Rye, will need horses to catch up to me."

"That is hare-brained," Brochfael snapped. "It will take you weeks on foot." He rolled his eyes. "I'll either find you a tame mare or just send Patrick. You can hide here."

Fists clenched at his sides, Harey sighed. "Listen. The fastest way is a line. The line from here to Bangor involves terrain too steep for a horse. I will steal a stallion from invaders in the valley, ride to the cliffs, set the horse free with my gratitude, and take another. I will need help with burials. Hang me when I get back. Now, sod off you fuckin' tarse so I can run."

Harey stomped to Maura. He flung his arm around her, bent to her ear, and his fear poured out in a frantic whisper. "He lives—my heart still beats. I need you. He needs you. It takes five days. Sleep little, you will be there in three or four, but do not kill the horse. Rye will beg. Deny him sharing your horse. He is too young to face a thousand dead. Braid your hair. Ride like a man. Patrick must come. He will kill any who would harm you. Promise!"

Maura worried her lip. She nodded into his hot stare and swallowed back a river of tears. He released her and turned to Owen. "Let Vina have your bow. She can hit a mark ten paces away. Watch over Bit for me. Hurry. Fetch your da from the far field."

Owen wiped his face and bolted. Harey plucked the leverets from his pocket, rushed inside, and dropped them on Maura's bed as she followed on his heels. She would return them to Bitty, then grab bread and a waterskin, and head out after him the moment fresh horses were ready.

The lord cleared his throat from the doorway. "You will not be hung for theft of a pagan's horse. Food from your chieftain's pantry is another matter. Despite the color, I know your sins. Bury Gareth for me and I will show leniency."

"Fuck. You." Harey snarled. He caught the waterskin Maura tossed him. "I will shove pretty yellow eggs up your arse if he is lying in a pool of blood because you ran him off."

"Harey!" Maura's heart didn't know in which direction to explode. Her Gareth dead or her Harey about to die.

Brochfael barked a laugh. "You have grown a spine, young hare. Much as you think me a tarse, I loved my brother. Find Gareth while I dispatch those who slaughtered unarmed monks. I want him buried with sanction and respect."

Harey spun to exit and Brochfael seized him. Maura's breath froze as the large man hugged him. "Gareth did tell me of this discord within the religions. Last year, he reinforced an underground exit, but his corpse will be out front, along the path they marched on." He shoved the lad from him and bowed his head as Harey disappeared.

"Underground exit?" Maura asked. "Then why, why are you sure that he—all of them are dead?"

Brochfael raised his chin, and Maura fought the rush of despair. He had tears on his cheeks. "Gareth has not accepted a white vestment. Love of a woman and the bastard he rescued deterred him from his vows. Before he watched a thousand fall, he would have turned killer. He will be on the front line, dead monks and enemy around him."

"Why, Brochfael, why? The missionary Gareth worried about, his curse came forth? The druids, their gods demanded the sacrifice of so many?"

Brochfael shook his head. "Augustin of Canterbury was but a smug, opinionated man grabbing at power through threats. He said if Welsh and Cornish churches did not make him archbishop and come to heel under his Roman thumb, preach charity and Christian life to the pagans, there would be death by pagan hands. The chieftains...I did not heed his words.

To shove the Roman version of salvation at those who care naught about blood lettings? Spread the word of a passive Christ to Saxons who have plundered and raided our homes for generations?"

Brochfael shrugged. His dark eyes filled with grief. "I wanted him safe, not to deprive you of years in his bed. Before I sent him to his death, my little brathair would not raise his bow to shoot a hare let alone kill a man. What else could I have done other than give him to the God who would allow him to keep his hands clean? I sacrificed Gareth. I now care for no man. He is in heaven. I head the other direction. Fare thee well."

Maura ran forward and flung her arms around him. "Then if it is hell you seek, go and avenge all the good monks with my blessing. Gareth loved...loves you, too. Nothing can take that from us."

Brochfael nodded. He eased from her arms. Without a backward glance, he mounted his horse, and the three men rode off to their fate while Maura hastened to hers.

∞

For three days and three nights, Maura rode hard and fast behind Patrick. He had decided to take the path veering to the east, miles out of their way, but they bypassed marauders who closed in on Brochfael at the passage of Dee. Plucked from the fields, there could have been but fifty men to ride with the lord. They faced the thousands who had massacred the monks alone, until other chieftains responded.

Brochfael, I rather hate you. Maura feared she would never again set eyes on the formidable elder brother who bowed to pagan and Roman beliefs, and lost the one soul he cared for.

Gareth, I love you. She feared even more she would

never find her lover, alive or dead. Locating one corpse amidst the ruins of the largest gathering of teachers and students in the known world would be a daunting task. If not for Vina and Owen, she would care naught if she returned. Surely deserters remained, looting the stored foods and whiskey barrels. Patrick could not drive a sword through them all, before they sent him and her to join Harey.

Harey, I love you. Maura's heart ached. Brochfael had sent a grief-stricken man to his certain death without hesitation, and she had done nothing to dissuade either of them.

"Your arse as sore as mine?" Patrick called back. "Where is our damn hare-loving freak of nature, anyway? We should have caught up to Harey long ago."

She forced a smile and shrugged. She had promised Cassie, Patrick's wife and surrogate mother to Maura, the big oaf would return to her. Cassie knew she lied. "He would have run until his legs gave out and then crawled. Horse or not, perhaps he is already there."

Patrick nodded and turned back to the path. "Sneakier than a fox, he will ride some unlucky sod's horse. By high noon on the morrow, we should catch up to him."

Hours later, she shivered under Patrick's arm as he slept. Daybreak would come too soon. She dreaded finding Harey, dead of a broken heart, curled beside the body of their one true love.

It was closer to mid-afternoon when they crested the high hill and closed in on the cathedral. Plumes of black smoke had shown them the way. Curved peaks and then the sea behind them, Gwynedd Wales had been a gorgeous locale to raise an abbey.

It now lay in ruins. Shattered towers, broken main archway, the horses shied from the bodies heaped everywhere along the long entrance pathway.

Hundreds of men, throats slit, chests gutted, their white robes stained red. Trumpets and prayer beads lay tumbled beside splayed fingers.

Patrick's shoulders hunched, his body wizened as they guided the horses through the stench of rotting flesh and entered the main circle of smoldering structures. Buildings had collapsed in on themselves, the fires burnt out in the steady drizzle of last eve's rain.

Patrick wept. Maura tried to, but a surreal haze fell upon her as image after image pounded into her. Every crumpled body wore Gareth's face, but Patrick did not stop and she followed his lead like a woman in a trance.

There did not seem to be a living thing other than them. No horses, dogs, cats hunting their owners. The stone cathedral was intact, black with soot from the torched interior. Patrick turned to the left, circling the huge area.

Around back, the gardens had escaped the flames. Emerald ivy grew thick and plush along wood trellis, bordering rows of trampled summer vegetables.

Patrick slowed. "Harey? Where are you, laddie?" he bellowed at the top of his lungs.

"Harey? Harey? Please, please, where—"

"There." Patrick gestured to the far end of the cathedral. A man stumbled out, carrying another.

Patrick leaped from his horse, dropped the reins, and ran. He reached to take the man and halted as Harey jerked backward.

"Dead go beside the potatoes. Get another." Harey's voice rang hollow, and Maura could barely hear him as she fell off her mare in a clumsy drop.

"Dead?" she gasped.

"Yes. Dead go outside." Harey stumbled forward toward the garden. "Dying, inside before the altar."

Please, did he say dying, not dead? Harey looked terrible, his blackened face drained of color. He had already marched under the largest trellis without a second glance at them. Maura yearned to grab him and sob until she was empty of every drop of water and blood within her, but she dragged her feet behind Patrick.

Through the wide archway, a hundred feet inside, charred wooden beams had been shifted aside to open the way into a small access room, a pantry of sorts. Planks lay partially charred, bags of grains overturned and burned, the rest looted. An entrance, into a tunnel large enough for a man to crawl through, gaped in the stone wall it had been hidden behind.

She dropped to her knees and fear raced up and down her spine. Six feet down into the darkness the opening widened. An underground room. Dim outlines of what had to be bodies lay beside each other. On his hands and knees, Patrick tugged one backward by the heels. He crawled to the side, leaving the still form in front of her. "Drag him out. I felt his chest rise. Try not to bang his head too much."

Maura snapped her mouth closed. This was someone's son, soon dead from dehydration and shock most likely. Outrage gave her strength as she crouched lower. She grabbed filthy feet and scuttled backward while Patrick crawled forward to lean over another.

Outside the pantry, on the cold stone pavement, she could not lift the man and she feared if she pulled him down the stone outside, or along the steps into the church she would finish him off. Tears welled, nausea churned, and she fought her dry heave. A jagged wound in his arm, bone exposed, he would most likely not survive regardless.

A quivering hand on her shoulder raised her gaze. Feral and blank, Harey's dark gaze was unfathomable. "Living go to the room with the big cross. There is water. Can you carry him?" He lowered his hand to her.

She shook her head. Tears burst free and she took his hand. He pulled her to her feet and grasped her shoulders. "Be strong. Too many need help." He released her and turned to Patrick, a young man in his arms. "Dead?"

"Not yet." Patrick jerked his chin at the hole. "Fetch another, sweetheart. Harey and me will bring them to the grave or not."

Maura could not breathe or speak. She pleaded with her eyes for Patrick to say the words.

He turned to Harey gathering up the unconscious man she had dragged out. "Find him yet?"

His jaw dropped. A hot light filled his eyes. "Pardon! I thought I told you. I—I am talking aloud now, right?" His expression was dazed. Streaked with blood, his arms trembled from the weight of the man he held. Harey looked so confused.

Patrick nodded. "Yes, laddie. We are really here. And Gareth?"

Harey jerked his chin toward the interior. "He still breathed since I placed two in the garden. Come."

The ringing stopped, her vision cleared, and Maura felt her heart beat for the first time in days. Harey stumbled past her, toward the large columns into the wide area with the sun streaming through the jagged remains of huge, stained-glass windows.

Gareth! She had, she just had to look upon his face. The exhaustion fled from her limbs, Maura hurried after Harey and Patrick and into the light.

No longer filtered by sheets of glass, shards scattered everywhere, the setting sun shot rays throughout the huge cathedral. Thirty plus men lay beneath the burned remnants of the crucified god.

Most still, some moving, two sat up and gulped water.

Harey settled his burden down and headed for the kettle filled with water. He flicked his fingers to the right.

In a pool of light off to the side, Gareth lay on his back, his head pillowed by white linen. A fallen angel, his blond hair had been combed like a halo about his shoulders.

Maura ran. Her knees smacked wood. She leaned and brushed her lips to his. Cold. Still. Nothing. *Gareth, please!* She slapped her fingers on his chest— the rise and fall so shallow she could barely feel it. She pressed harder, her lips molded to his.

Rough hands grabbed her from behind.

Harey yanked her to her feet. "He needs air. Can you...there are more men who may drink. Gareth will not. Please? Help the others?"

"Of course," Maura mumbled. "Sorry. Harey—I love you. Thank you for finding him for us." She turned from Harey's blank eyes and imagined claws ripping her heart from her chest and tossing it before the god.

She headed back to hell.

Each time she pulled another man out, either Patrick or Harey nodded to answer her unspoken question. Gareth continued to breathe.

When five more lay inside the worship area and a dozen in the garden, Maura hated herself for the relief she felt as she crawled the underground room and found it empty. Why had the handful of men who escaped the sword not continued through the narrow tunnel and into the woods? She suspected Harey had dragged each man hundreds of feet and lined them up before he began sorting dead from living. He had also somehow shifted those beams to find the entrance in the pantry.

She heaved a heavy body into the light and

collapsed. All the men in this hole looked no older than Gareth, most barely in their twenties. None that she had touched wore white, all were filthy. She tenderly brushed dirt from the man's face and raised her gaze to Patrick.

He lifted her to her feet. "He's the last? Dead?"

"Yes." Her legs would not work. She leaned on his arm and nodded. "Why did they not flee into the hills?"

"Harey said the bastards found the exit in the far garden and piled hundreds of bodies on top to block it." Patrick gestured to the tunnel entry. "He used a horse and roped clothing together to move the beams."

Patrick swung his arm under her knees. "Come do something womanly with Harey. He must rest. The lad is really hurting, as are we all. Ribs broken, Gareth has a huge knot on the back of his skull. We cannot seem to rouse him." He walked with the gait of a beaten man and with every step Maura fought her fear. *Please, please, please, any god that listens, give me my heart back.*

Harey bent over Gareth. His lips did not lower to press in a loving kiss, he scowled. Fury creased his brow. He cradled Gareth's head and shoved a pewter cup to his mouth. "Fuckin' sod. Wake up and drink before I kill you myself. It has been hours. How long do I wait? Why will you not look at me? Bastard. Please?"

"Put me down," Maura whispered to Patrick.

She stumbled to her men and huddled on the other side of Gareth. She reached across his chest, his brown robe opened to expose deep, dark bruising, and took the cup from Harey. She drew her arm back and threw the water into Gareth's face. Drops splattered onto Harey's arm.

His jaw dropped. "Why did you do that? He has to drink. Get more water."

"Shh...Do not...." Gareth's soft words, more of a

moan, trailed off. Through the ringing in her ears, she could not be sure she had really heard them.

"Gareth?" Harey and Maura yelped at the same time.

His eyelids fluttered, trying to lift thick droplets, but his eyes did not open. His tongue shot out and licked his cracked lip, and Maura gasped her joy. She brushed his cheek, Harey hit her fingers away, and Patrick loomed over them.

"Fight over him later," Patrick said. "Maura, shove your finger between his lips. Harey, run your hand over his throat, force him to swallow." Patrick tipped water into Gareth's mouth as Maura smiled all her love at Harey, and he did the same back at her.

Chapter Eight

*H*arey tugged his rancid tunic over his throbbing head. Every part of his body ached. His legs trembled as if he had run across Briton instead of the mile from the abbey, and he did not hesitate. On the deepest side of the river, he launched himself off the bank.

Cool water stung his cheeks, slapped his chest, and the weight of his dirt-laden pants tugged him down, down, down. The fresh water stream ran strong, gurgling happily to the sea. Thanks to thick fields of snow thawing the past spring, constant summer rains, the area had been blessed with water and cursed with blood.

Images of an ashen face flitted behind his eyelids. It had been a week since he had carried Gareth from the tunnel, but he had yet to fully awaken to the pain of broken ribs, cracked skull, and the fever of a man who had been buried alive for days. He could do no more than swallow sopped bread and water, while dreaming and murmuring names.

Harey's heart clenched. He had yet to hear his—the name Gareth had given him—fall from Gareth's lips.

No matter how hard he scrubbed his flesh, how deep he went, how long he allowed himself to stay under cleansing waters, he feared his mind would remain filthy and furious.

He hated the religions.

He hated the man he loved for bowing to pagan and to Rome.

He hated himself for not understanding anything.

Why had a blood-hungry Christ not smote blood-drenched Saxons? How could men kill unarmed men so mercilessly? Why did Harey dread returning to Brochfael's keep, fearing spring would find his own blood soaking the ground? But even if a coward was sacrificed for the greater good, how could virgin blood ensure a harvest to be bounteous?

Harey expected Gareth's brother no longer lived, but his demise only meant another would seize power. Unless either tarse, Colin or Argos, survived and rallied the remaining villagers to secure the area, Brochfael's territory would eventually be overrun by a neighboring chieftain. With crops destroyed or confiscated by marauders, the desperate and hungry would be even more eager to appease Eostre.

Harey kicked upward, and then sank until he floated a foot below the surface. He wanted to hide in the darkness as long as possible. A bastard taken in by a good man, he should jump from the depths, eager and happy to embrace his fate. His throat slit could ensure Gareth, Maura, Patrick, and the handful of Christ followers sheltering in these ruins would find food to survive another winter.

The Saxons had made certain of their bounty with Eostre, no doubt of that. Pockets of smoldering wood surrounded the abbey, live sparks beneath the heaps of ash, despite last night's rains. Roughly a hundred bodies remained, stacked alongside each other and waiting for burial. Harey and Patrick, four men from Bangor, and five of the stronger survivors had been digging graves for six days.

After they had lain to rest an older man beaten so badly no one knew his name, prayer beads merged into his flesh from clenching them, his robe reeking of piss and decay from his skin, Patrick insisted Harey quit for the day.

Harey had gone to stare at the rise and fall of Gareth's chest. Then he attacked the gardens. Weeded and filled a tattered basket. Returned to see Gareth breathed. He left to place the vegetables in the remains of the kitchen for Maura to smash and stew so ill men could easily swallow and ran back to Gareth, still breathing. He had heard Maura's footsteps. No fool, Harey raced the opposite direction, not stopping until he reached this creek. Finally, the stench of rotted flesh no longer clogged his nostrils, but his chest had started to burn. Felt good, not breathing.

The rough hands taking him from behind, not so much.

Fear filled him. Would his death, without ceremony, still please Eostre? Yanked to the surface, flipped onto his back, water sprayed aside. A powerful arm slung over his throat, a large man dragged him as he sputtered.

"Let—let go!" Harey gasped.

"Hell, no. I—you all right, then?" The man did not give him a chance to answer. He heaved their bodies forward, thrusting Harey ahead of him onto the creek's edge, and then splashed out and collapsed to the ground, gulping beside him.

Harey scrambled to his feet. Every muscle poised to run, he stared at the man sprawled in front of him.

The man coughed. He sat up. "Forgive me. I thought you had drowned."

"Oh. No. I breathe."

"Obviously. How the bloody hell can you stay under

that long? Gareth is right. You are not human." The man rubbed water from his eyelashes and drew his gaze up and down Harey.

"You know Gareth? He said I am...not a man?"

"Of course, and of course not. You are his Harey, and I know he thinks you are the man—or angel—or whatever raised by harts and hares. Thank you for saving my life. My name is Jonathon." He pushed sopping hair from his forehead. "You do not recognize me with my face cleaned. Maura let some of us out of the beds."

Harey blinked at the dark haired man. Every face, alive or dead, he had dragged from the tunnel looked up at him with vacant blue eyes, blond stubble on their cheeks. Even after he found Gareth, he had not been sure he really found him. In fact, he should leave now to see if Gareth had not disappeared or worse.

He tensed and then froze, ears perked. Clumsy feet trod, approaching from the south. He shifted his attention back to Jonathon and lowered his hand. "Someone...two at least, draw near."

Jonathon clasped his fingers and pulled back to his tug. A smile filled his face. The man as big as Gareth refused to get up. "Shh, lad. Not bloody Saxons, but friends that Maura commanded to wash thoroughly, minding behind our ears."

Stiffness drained from Harey's shoulders. A tall, sturdy man stumbled into the clearing, supporting a smaller hobbling on one foot.

"Found him," Jonathon called out.

"We are not blind." The taller man took in the scene. "Could not wait for us to go in?" He spun deep green eyes back at Harey.

"Harey! I'm Eadmar," the crippled man called out.

They stopped by the bank and Eadmar plodded down.

Green eyes eased closer. "I'm Cynric. Er...Gareth saved my life and you carried me from the grave. Thank you." He stuck his hand out.

Harey could not stop his flinch. *Cynric?* He had heard the name mumbled from Gareth's lips more times than he cared to count.

The extended hand faltered and Harey forced himself to take hold. A fast shake and he jerked loose.

"Please do not look at me like that." Cynric slumped. "Is Gareth finally awake? He told you about me? I am sorry. I—I love him. A sin, but I cannot help it."

Harey stepped back. "Gareth's fever broke last night, but he has said little other than calling your name. Love him? A sin? What...does that mean?"

Jonathon pushed to his feet. "Nothing. We all love the sorry sod. He kept chanting our names whenever we went quiet. Gareth broke his arm trying to dig through and then the rock whacked his skull. I heard Cynric finally stop whining. His name would have been the final one Gareth mumbled before his voice gave out. Or before I did, cannot remember."

"I was not—"

"Yes, you were." Eadmar snickered at Cynric. "Now me, I was as brave as a bairn. Gareth sang me a lullaby, and that terrible sound was the last I heard until the most wondrous notes. Not my mum, but Maura murmuring like an angel for me to waken and drink before she spilled more water down my chin."

Harey faced Cynric's stare. He wished he wore more than the thin pants clinging to his legs. The man drew a deep breath. "You want to know about it?"

"Yes." Harey angled his backside away from them.

Cynric shifted his sight beyond the murmuring creek. "Screaming outside, fire everywhere, murderers had not reached the kitchens. Gareth told the dozen of us there to exit the back, try for the trees. When he did not do as he said, I stayed with him. He hunted and found a knife. I grabbed another and followed him toward the nearest flames, the cathedral.

"Four brothers, who surrounded Eadmar and Jonathon like guards, ran out. They commanded us with them, led us to the tunnel, and threw Eadmar and Jonathon inside. Brother Sebastian told Gareth and me to guard the entrance while they attempted another sweep of the rooms. He said they had gathered roughly a hundred students so far, and to stop any monk wishing to join them instead of God.

"Five minutes, sounds of slaughter closing in, only the four monks returned. They seized Gareth, forced him to his knees, and thrust him into the dark hole. In a white robe, I was not destined to follow but Gareth crawled out, yelling there was room and for them all to get in. He grabbed for me, and Christ help me, I did not release his hand. Brother Sebastian called Gareth an idiot. Said someone must hide the entrance. He knocked me over, on top of Gareth. I pinned him, punched him, and he went still. I dragged him as far from the entrance as praying students allowed, yelling for everyone to be silent as the dead. We watched the light disappear as they sealed off the opening."

Jonathon and the man with the broken foot joined Cynric in looking to the distance. The grief on their faces told Harey they had not heard this before.

Eadmar hunched over. "Brother Sebastian was a good man."

"Yes," Cynric whispered. "He saved you from me six months ago and let Gareth rescue me, a monster who should be burning with every Saxon ever born."

Jonathon slapped him on the shoulder. "Arsehole. Be still. How many times does Eadmar forgive you? Forget your sins and pay homage. That is the man himself over there. The warrior who freed us from the earth."

The three turned to stare at Harey, and he felt the heat fill his face.

Jonathon grinned. "I am good. I paid my debt." He flexed his arms, posturing for Cynric and Eadmar. "I just saved our hero from drowning. Gareth will be so happy when he wakes. Christ, how long can that arse sleep?"

Harey managed to close his gaping mouth as Jonathon smirked at his friends. "Not a day passed when Gareth did not tell stories. He will love me the best, knowing I saved his Harey while you two dallied in the field."

Cynric arched his brows at Harey. "In the shadow of a thousand graves, you allow a liar to stand?"

What? I should do something?

"Take him, Harey. Go on," Eadmar muttered.

His legs willing, his mind confused, he leaped. He hit Jonathon in the shoulder, grasped his elbow, and hefted him upward. The big man barely stumbled, hopped into the river, and splashed down onto his arse.

"Bastard." He laughed. The sound rang hollow into Harey's ears, bouncing off the dappled water toward the sky. *He knows I am ill-begotten? Seriously?*

An imaginary, loving hand hit him upside the head. The beloved voice of a blond angel murmured inside his head. *"No, my silly lad, he teases you like a brother."*

Jonathon stood, pulled off his tunic, and tossed it on the bank. He stomped farther in, fell to his knees, and pushed off for deeper water.

Harey turned and his lungs locked. Cynric and Eadmar tried to hide their gawking. Silence from behind him, and he knew the scars on his bared back were now being examined by Jonathon. He fought his shiver, the knots in his stomach tightening.

Face flushed, Cynric took hold of Eadmar and helped him remove his tunic.

"Jump in, Harey-lad." Jonathon chuckled. "I will make sure you stay afloat." He lay on his back, splashing like a downed hart as he peeled off woolen pants.

Stripped naked, Cynric hefted Eadmar into the creek and Harey shuffled his feet. Was he to undress completely? Let them stare at the branding on his arse as well?

Gareth was the only man who knew it all. Three years ago, he had rubbed salve on Harey every morn for two weeks. He said as he grew the damage would eventually fade from skin and mind. Then Maura came upon them and Gareth hurried to cover Harey. Later, he claimed to be wrong. He said he did not want the welts gone, he loved every inch of them, and he had best leave them be. Harey understood he had given up, weary of the ugliness.

Mind and body, he would always be broken. Had Gareth moved his strong hands onto Cynic? The man was so beautiful. His voice could be the one to bring Gareth around.

"Harey?"

He blinked. Jonathon came into focus.

"Wondering about Gareth?"

He nodded.

"After you check on him, come tell us when we can sneak past Maura to look upon him ourselves."

"Promise?" Eadmar called out.

"You will never see this tunic again if you do not." Cynric stood, waist deep. He had abandoned Eadmar for Harey's tunic. He pounded at it, dipping it into the water. "And Harey? Gareth slept alone at the abbey, until the bloody pagans came and you and Maura joined us. He has snored in your bed too long. Yell in his ear. The lazy arse should be in this river with us."

Harey's smile leaped from his heart to his face. He ran.

Two miles disappeared, the creek falling away behind him faster than a blue eye could wink if lids would only lift. With years of practice, the clumsy grace of an animal on two callused feet instead of four, he slowed to a soft, soundless trot. He bypassed the mounds of dead men, curving past the main trellis toward the back entrance of the abbey.

In the freshly weeded garden, Maura bent. Her long braid was fluttering in the soft breeze, and she wrestled with a fat potato plant.

A good man would go help her, instead of filling his mind with the curves of her small arse, jealous lust dancing down his chest, through his gut, and into his loins.

A bad man would not make his presence known. He would slink, a wolf around her, creep into the blackened ruins, and pad down the carcass remains of a hallway to steal a precious moment alone with the angel she loved.

On a firm pallet, in a section of the abbey that managed to survive what hundreds of men did not, Gareth lay flat, long lashes curled against his ashen cheeks.

Harey fell to his knees beside the bed. "Gareth...do you love a man of God? Would Cynric's hand upon your brow arouse you?" He unclenched his fists. "My regrets. The touch of a heathen bastard is all you get in this moment."

As he reached for the strip of white linen beside the bowl of fresh water, the sound of the rise and fall of Gareth's chest ceased.

No! I do not care who you love. You cannot, shall not die on me. He twisted his head around so fast his vision blurred. He blinked hard.

Wounded blue eyes stared up at Harey as if...as if he were a big man come to rescue Gareth from the darkest hell.

His tongue thickened, his heart could no longer beat, his body about to explode with relief—and surprise. In a heartbeat, three years fell from his mind. Memory slammed into him, the sounds and scents of the past. Splattering cascade of falling water, crisp air tainted by the presence of a malevolent witch, the thrum of a released arrow flying to stab into his calf. Except, in this moment, the arrow pierced his heart and love and longing rushed up his throat as confusion flooded Gareth's gaze.

"Is...it...really...?" Gareth rasped the words out as if his chest was on fire.

Did he not know who Harey was? Could the man have lost his mind? He had taken a cruel blow to the head. The touch of a hand, solid and firm, might help to show he existed. He reached.

Gareth flinched.

Harey froze. It took all his will, but he dropped his hand.

Gareth's mouth opened. Closed. Opened. "Real? Har...Harey?"

Harey swallowed hard. "Yes. You wish Maura? She is here in the garden." He readied to hop to his feet. His limbs locked as Gareth's large hand, as weak as a bairn's, fluttered out.

There was no halting Harey's reaction. Stronger than any magnetic rock known to man, the pull grasping him came from the depths of whatever soul he had. As if those fingers were his salvation, he leaned closer and his heartbeat stuttered when Gareth's limp hand wrapped around his wrist. If only the man did not look so frightened.

Gareth dragged his gaze up and down Harey's bare chest as he mumbled, "Why...why are you in hell?"

"Pardon?"

"Fire, smoke, and then gone. Blood, darkness, cold, thirst...." The ball in Gareth's throat went up and down. "You...I do not want you here! Please...God...."

A fist squeezed Harey's heart. "Gareth, you are not in heaven or hell or dreaming. You are still at the home of a fallen Christ. Shh. Do not stress yourself. You wish me gone? Maura will explain. She...Gareth?"

He jerked his grip away and snorted. "I do not believe you." He started to shove his body upward.

Harey shot to his feet. He grasped Gareth's shoulders and pushed him flat. "Your ribs are broken. Be still."

"I cannot. Real or not, if any murdering bastard dares to touch my Harey...you...I must—"

"You must listen." *His Harey? How I love those words.* "Do not try. I will not let you up." He felt his smile curving wider and wider. "The only bastard doing any touching will be me. The Saxons are gone. You are safe. I am real. Do you understand?"

Gareth sighed. His lower lip trembled. "No. Please. Hold...kiss me?"

The world stopped. A babe to the teat, a hare to a carrot, a man to a man, Harey lowered his head. He brushed his lips against Gareth's.

Gentle, soft, careful—an intense hunger seized him. He fought the urge, gave a careful peck, and struggled to keep from collapsing over the wounded man. He could...would...must stop his mouth from pressing, diving, merging into Gareth's. The tip of his tongue yearned to shoot out, gobble, taste, and plunder. Blood drained from his head, pounding through his veins in a rush to harden his cock aching to roll against, batter into, kiss along the other cock but inches away.

The sound of a laden basket hitting the floor penetrated the din of lust fogging his head.

"Harey?" Maura's cool whisper danced on the air behind him.

Self-hatred roared within. It exploded outward, bouncing from one scar to another along his exposed back. His face on fire, he staggered aside.

She did not even look upon his guilt. Her sights were on Gareth's eyes finally open, flooded with bemused awareness, his tongue licking reddened lips.

Maura ran forward. The joy bursting from her gaze could fill a man's heart—if he had one.

Chapter Nine

The sun slowly sank, coloring the horizon with burning shades of red and warning Maura that another long summer day neared an end. The sliver of the barely visible moon provided little light, meaning she must hurry. It would be miraculous to have some sort of device that captured light, releasing its fire with more precision than a torch or candle, which could be capped off to store the energy as needed.

A grim smile played on her lips as she strode from the kitchen. A circle of survivors determined to regain the camaraderie they shared in better times had inspired her to occasionally dwell on something other than how blessed this fall's harvest at the monastery would be, the garden overflowing with vegetables nourished by hundreds of decomposing bodies.

The handful of Gareth's friends not struggling with serious injury took turns resting from the formidable task of rebuilding to sit with him. The more vocal demanded he not dwell on nightmares, but help solve their latest philosophical wonder to pass the time during which he could do little but lay on his backside. Gareth would sigh, wince as he arched his brows as if even his eyelashes hurt, and tell them to sod off. That the only thing speeding his recovery was the sight of Harey and Maura, not bothersome idealists who expected him to think as well as heal. Naturally his words did naught but encourage disheartened students to continue engaging him despite the fact exhaustion lined their faces.

In the little bedroom they had made as comfortable as possible, the stumps of oak turned into makeshift chairs were empty. Only one man graced the room and her stomach clenched, lust and love pooling inside her at the sight of Gareth, fast asleep.

So beautiful—my man—my love. His blond braids shone brighter than any king's crown forged of gold, freshly washed and plaited this morn by Harey's loving fingers. The thick woolen tunic was stretched too tightly across his chest, but one of the few found to be free of blood and urine stains. His face slack and peaceful, every inch of bruised and flawless skin had been gently sponged by her and Harey at daybreak.

And now, as night drew close, she wished to do some not-so-gentle cleansing of her own skin. A solid scrub in the fresh waters of the creek, and maybe she would see the spark return to Gareth's gaze when she rested beside him.

She quietly stepped to the corner. Beside the water bowl sat their hoarded ball of soap, a precious acquisition in the rural areas of Briton. She had heard rumors of a new soap guild within London, where the fortunate populace could barter for interesting combinations of scents. The soap she tucked into the pocket of her tunic had been made of animal fat, beech tree ash, and goat milk. She had been pleasantly surprised to find she could salvage hunks out of the melted mess in the ruins of the storage area. It seemed the Saxons were more interested in the sacks of grains and barrels of whiskey, instead of the means to cleanse an ocean of blood from their skin.

A bear about to embark on a hunt without the slumbering cub, a bird hopping off the eggs to perch on the edge of the nest, a wolf leaving her den unguarded could not feel more apprehensive than she, but she hardened her resolve. A lass had a goddess-given right to cleanliness, and she wished a proper wash of her hair this night. She tightened the sash of the clothing that had belonged to a slender monk, the stain of his blood now familiar, and readied to slip from the room. Another glance at her lover, his chest rising and falling in deep sleep, gave her pause.

The knowledge of how close she had come to losing Gareth continuously shook her to the core, and she thought of the other man beyond beautiful to her. *So grateful—mine—whether he knows or cares.* Forget deities, pagan or Christian. She owned an eternal debt to Harey.

Midday, when he had grabbed a chunk of bread and departed to continue working with Patrick, the lines in his forehead, tightly pressed lips showed her that despite the burials finished, the task of clearing charred timber and rubble was hard on a lad who should be running, frolicking in the forest with his pets, and stealing eggs for hungry children.

It had been eight wonderful, difficult, joyous, exhausting, and worrisome days since he had persuaded Gareth to break free of his unconsciousness. She had witnessed the sweet brush of lips between the pair. She had also seen the guilt fill Harey's face before happiness vanished all thought of anything other than the knowledge Gareth had awakened with awareness in his eyes.

Not many with broken arm and ribs could have survived that long without water, as well as a horrific blow to the head which could have left him damaged beyond repair. And now she had to take action before they rested this night, and Gareth inched further and further away from her, preferring a freshly bathed Harey.

So doing this—my body— my soul reeks of death. She bent to the pallet she had claimed, pushed aside for the day, lifted it, and wrapped her fingers around the handle of the weapon Patrick had given her. She straightened and awkwardly tucked the short dagger with a broad, tapering, double-edged blade into her sash.

A fool's errand to head for the creek on her own, and one sure to earn her a nonstop scolding if any of the forty-five men working diligently to heal this cursed abbey understood she had fled their watchful protection. Not that she cared about any squawking from a brotherhood who flushed and stammered whenever the lone female in their midst lost her smile, but if anything did happen to her, Gareth would...she sighed. At least he would have Harey to comfort him.

One last peek to insure Gareth was breathing peacefully, she left the door ajar. She walked past the rooms not yet repaired to stop and knock on a newly replaced door. Broken in spirit not body, James—who hailed from a village in Wessex—had risen before dawn to begin scraping a meal together for the rest of them.

"Come in," he said and she eased the door open. He smiled at her and pushed to his feet from where he had been kneeling beside his pallet. "Gareth fares well?"

"Yes. Sleeping. I am sneaking off to the creek. Would you listen, go to him if he calls out?"

"Of course." Worry filled his gaze. He ducked his head. "You are not bathing alone, right?"

She swallowed her sigh. "Harey has dragged a dozen more trees from the forest. He will be glad to stop for the day."

James shifted from foot to foot. "He is very good with the axe against wood. I am not sure he..." the large man flushed. "May I go with you, instead?"

She grinned. "What if I decide this tunic is a hindrance when wet?"

The color in his cheeks grew.

"I but tease you," she said. "Perhaps Patrick, Jonathon or Cynric wish to watch a woman rinse her hair using more than a bucket of water. I best hasten. Thank you for easing Gareth's mind if he wonders where I am."

He nodded. "Leave the door open."

On the forest side of the ruins, the group including Patrick hefted the axe constantly. Support beams, planks for the roof, furniture, so much needed to be replaced or repaired. He hoped to soon surprise Gareth with his first attempt at making a rocking chair. Gareth was already pushing himself to sit and his ribs would heal faster if the big fool had more support than a rough stump.

Her heart sank after she crossed the large field and closed in on the huge pile of stacked timber. The expected cluster of men was gone. They had finished removing the branches on the trees dragged out yesterday, and Harey must have needed all hands to carry and rope more to his warhorse. They would be harvesting the selected trees in the forest now.

Bloody hell. Perchance if she stopped walking as slow as a slug, she could finish and return in time to have a dozen men escort her back to Gareth. She picked up the pace, a direct beeline into the woods.

It took her what seemed like hours, but finally the fast-flowing wide creek tumbling down the hills to become a river which emptied into the sea came into view. A fast look round did not expose any creature, man or beast, lurking. She wished a woman or two or ten would ease out from around the trees.

Surrounded by men healing from the atrocities of other men was not easy. They all slept in rooms as close to each other as they could manage in the ruins. Survivors bathed and wiped the arses of their brothers with broken arms, but looked to her to wake the lads who wept in their sleep, crying out for their mums. It was a burden she would shoulder without complaint, but no longer with streaks of sweat, piss, and vomit in her long thick hair.

She clutched the dagger hilt, eased it from her side, and dropped it to the ground. The too-large tunic followed, bumps of cold breaking out on her skin. She pulled loose the strip of linen from her hair, retrieved the soap from the tunic pocket, and stood on the brink of what promised to be bone-shivering cold water.

Jump in all at once from the middle rock? Or one easy step at a time?

The decision was taken from her. The soap went flying from her fingers and the air slammed from her lungs as her body hit the dirt. A heavy hand landed on the back of her head, her face smashed into the wet soil of the creek bank. The scream lodged in her throat, unable to summon the air to escape. The weight on top of her forced her so hard into the ground, she feared her back was about to break.

"Attempt to call out, you will feel my fists as well as my cock." Low and rough, the man's voice sent fear pulsating within her from head to toe. "You wish to breathe without a gag, stay silent."

She did not, could not move and death would soon take her as she suffocated. Metallic and sharp, blood filled her mouth from where she had bitten her cheek. She worked her face against the ground and swallowed hard. Nausea intensified as blood slid down her throat. The browns of the moist dirt meeting gray dappled water became blurred, blackness edging her vision.

"Not a sound, understand?" The man eased his weight upward, and she managed to gulp a shallow mouthful of air. Anger, futile and thick filled her veins. She recognized the voice of the man sitting on her backside, fumbling with his breeches. Not a stranger, not a Saxon, but one of two brothers from the nearby village who had not gone after the invaders who had bypassed their homes, intent only on slaughtering the monks. Instead of avenging the dead, they had offered to help with repairs in exchange for food. She had placed bread, water and soup in front of him for the past three days.

"Bradyn...please. Let me up. I beg—"

His slap to the side of her head dimmed her sights again, sharp hurt exploding from ear to ear. She could barely hear anything other than the hot drum of her frightened heartbeat. She realized what was to come. Not just rape, he would most likely strangle her and then join the grieving men in blaming a Saxon straggler for her death.

Gareth—I am so sorry. His heart already broken, she did not know how he would go on.

Vina, Patrick, Cassie...and Harey. If only she had opened her heart to Harey. Given him her blessing to love as he pleased. His arms around Gareth, their arms around each other could have made all the difference to survive her loss.

The monster, on top of her, suddenly stiffened. Will to fight replaced petrified panic as he pushed off her and stood. She managed to smack her hand flat to the ground, readying to scramble onto her knees. The cruel whack of his foot knocked her back in place.

"Stay still, bitch. What is—"

Her arms came to life and she shoved herself up— only to kiss the ground as the man standing beside her toppled, pressing her flat.

No air, no hope—yes air, yes hope. Two men rolled off her.

She twisted around to see Harey on top. Bradyn was almost as large as Gareth. A nasty grin on his face, the bastard used his weight to flip Harey beneath him.

"Maura—run! Go," Harey bellowed.

She pushed to her feet and did as she was told.

"You sodden fool of a lad. Want my cock in you as well?"

As she halted and bent to her tunic, Maura listened to the smack of flesh hitting flesh.

She straightened and turned to see Bradyn jerk Harey up by the hair and punch him in the face. His arm rose again and she moved faster than she ever had in her life.

No hesitation. She used both hands to shove the dagger into the man's thick neck. It hurt, the ache vibrating up her arm and into her chest. Blood sprayed, hot and rancid hitting her in the face, throat, and breasts. Harey's wide eyes stared up at her, dark and stunned. The old wound on his forehead had cracked open. More blood seeped from his swollen lip.

Bradyn gurgled, drowning in his blood. He started to collapse over Harey, but Maura grabbed his shoulder. "Do not die on top of him!" She shoved him over. "Die on the ground like the dirt that you are."

Her heart pounded hard and fast, the beat of a warrior and the rage of a killer bursting through her veins. She reached down, Harey grasped her hand, and she yanked him to his feet. His arm wrapped around her shoulders and he spun them both aside. The feel of his trembling body, his muscles on edge and poised to flee—her bravado collapsed into that of bewildered prey who had taken down a predator by pure chance.

"Oh sweet goddess, bloody Christ, Harey—I just

killed a man."

"Yes, you did." He eased free of her, wiping blood from his lip.

The harsh sob welling inside Maura threatened to turn into a wail. She clenched her empty hands into fists. "And sodden hell, I dropped my soap in the creek."

He shied from looking at her, and she crossed her arms over her breasts. She swallowed hard and forced her aching legs to carry her to the tunic. She pulled it over her head and down. After she had tightened the sash, Harey finally raised his chin. The sight of his battered face made her heart crack. "I am sorry," she whispered.

He snorted. "I am not. Even if you did not belong to Gareth, no one has a right to take you like that." He sighed. "Are you hurt badly? That bastard weighs as much as a horse. Your back must be sprained." Any attempt at hardness fell from his expression. "I should have gotten here faster."

"You saved my life."

"And you mine." Harey narrowed his eyes. "I told you to run. Foolish woman. Can you imagine Gareth burying you, as well as all his friends?"

Maura bristled. "More foolish man, you think he would grieve you less than me?"

"His lass, his love, he would never recover."

"His lad, his love, his eyes fill with happiness the moment he sees you."

"You must be blind as Bitty's newborn kits. That hot light in blue eyes is not happiness, but irritation he is no longer alone with you."

"Are you totally daft? He...." Maura paused as Harey slumped. He stared at Bradyn, the blood pouring in a steady trickle from his neck to saturate the dirt.

"I should have been the one to kill him," he mumbled. "A man would have. Gareth has no reason to be proud of me."

A wave of exhaustion filled her. "You are as dense as these trees. Gareth is so filled with admiration, gratitude, and need for you...." Pain squeezed her chest. "When he sees your face, he will be furious—with me."

"But Gareth is not an arse to think being attacked like that could be your fault." Harey straightened and his voice grew rough. "I hate this world. Women cannot bath in peace. Men cannot pray to their god in peace. And a horse thief cannot chop up trees in peace. Perhaps Patrick has freed my friend from the ropes and he will consent to help us."

A low and harsh whistle blasted from Harey's lips. He glanced at the dead man. "I do not wish to carry him."

"Carry him?"

Harey nodded. "Unless we make the corpse disappear, leaving it to seem as if he abandoned his family, his brother will want to take the body to the village. Bradyn has...had a wife and two bairns."

Maura felt her heart plummet to her toes.

Harey rubbed his fingers across his bruised jaw. "It does not seem possible a man who would hurt a woman could be a good da. My mum must have been happy that my da deserted her. But I always wondered if he had not run, the women would have cooked him up into stew."

Maura's lips twitched. "I know you, who rarely eat meat of any sort, do not wish us to hide this body in such a sickening way. I best tell the truth. I killed him and I have no regrets."

The low sounds of hoofs thudding closer and closer reached her ears. The large warhorse Harey had stolen whinnied as he cleared the forest and trotted up to them.

Harey stepped forward, reaching to stroke the horse nuzzling into his shoulder. He turned to Maura. "He will help us with ease. Arion is used to blood. It is living men who beat him that he objects to." He rubbed behind the horse's ear and she found her gaze drawn to the corpse. His breeches loose around his hips, the stench of urine assaulted her as well as his cooling blood. Weariness trembled through Maura's limbs, and she closed her eyes.

I killed a human. Did that mean the Christ, whom Gareth had spent the past three years praying to, would have nothing to do with her?

I killed a father. No virgin, a bad man, would Eostre, bloated with the blood of good and pious monks, also think her sacrifice to be worthless?

I killed a husband. This life, the here and now with Gareth may be all a killer like her would have. Forget the afterlife. Time to make a solemn vow to herself in this blood-saturated moment. *I will see Gareth bound to me, husband to wife come spring, or another man will die.*

But what if after all that has happened, Gareth insisted he must commit to the Christ? Could she compete against dead monks who prayed for him to join them in heaven after his death?

She swallowed hard. She would just have to take on a multitude of slaughtered men, Christ, Eostre, Gareth's brother and her liege lord, the entire Saxon population. A murderer now, a woman to be reckoned with—she yelped like a frightened lass as a large hand clasped her arm.

She blinked, peering up into sweet brown eyes. A cool cloth, the strip of linen soaked in the water, caressed her cheek and a soft sob burst from her lips.

"Shh," whispered Harey. He scrubbed the blood from her face. "There is nothing to fear. I will stand by you. Always." The soiled cloth pushed into his pocket, he released her and stepped away. A sharp yank pulled the dagger from Bradyn's throat. Harey wiped it on the ground and then stuck it through the cord around his waist. He bent to gather up the body.

"Can I help?"

"I have him." He slung the man face down over the horse's back. He used the ropes lying across the horse to fasten the body to the animal. "Let us walk. Arion will follow."

"It is almost dark. I can run." The sun had set, the sky blackened, and it felt like shadows were clawing out from the trees to surround them.

She clearly saw the strong hand Harey held out to her. "I will make sure you do not step on a snake."

She tucked her fingers in his. "I had not thought of snakes before now."

He guided her forward. "You wish the dagger back? You use it well."

"I wish to never let go of you, at least until the morrow."

"Then our arms will rest across Gareth's chest. Come sunup, I will release you and jump out the window."

"Good plan. Broken ribs or not, if our Gareth understands the cut on your lip was from a fist, he will scream and swear and stagger from the bed to strangle a dead man." She swallowed against the big lump stuck in her throat. They walked in comfortable silence until they reached the field, Harey matching his pace to hers and the horse quietly following.

Harey drew them to a halt. She followed his gaze. Large forms approached and he tightened his grip on her hand. "Six men. That big one..." he bent forward, squinting, "do not fear. It is Patrick and friends."

Good goddess, how could he see? Perchance it could be the foods he ate not only strengthened long and muscular legs, but helped him as well to see like a hare hiding in the dark from winged hunters. She should gobble carrots, turnips and potatoes like the man pulling her faster and faster did.

"That you, laddie? Maura, too?" Patrick's loud voice called out. "That fearsome horse would not let her ride?"

"Yes and no," Harey yelled back. He stayed his feet, holding her close beside him. "Maura and I prefer to walk." He bent to her ear and whispered, "Let me lie to them like a man would. You got to kill that arsehole. Grant me this at least."

"No," she snapped. "You will not...ouch!" He had kicked at her ankle. A hard squeeze of her hand warned her more abuse was to come. She tried to tug loose. He would not let go. She lowered her voice to hiss. "If you dare to claim his blood—"

"Maura is in shock," Harey said as the shadows surrounded them and morphed into men. "She found Bradyn dead by the creek. A blade in his neck, a weapon like the one you gave her, Patrick. I was so surprised...I tripped. Cut my face on the rocks. We ask help. Patrick, you should carry Maura. Jonathon, you should carry me."

The men laughed and she huffed. "I am not in shock. I can walk."

"Shh, lassie." The largest shadow seized her. Next thing she knew, her feet left the ground and her head rested against Patrick's chest.

"Arses, all of you," she said. "Like I have not seen a dead man before. And, Patrick, do not listen to Harey. He—"

"He is a man to be trusted." It was the voice of

Cynric interrupting her. "All Saxons carry shield, sword, axe, and dagger. The murdering coward either ran when Maura approached or did not have the strength to pull the blade from Bradyn's fat neck. The man's brother will be pleased he died fighting our enemies."

Jonathon cleared his throat. "Bradyn's wife has washed clothing in exchange for bread and meat ever since I have been at the abbey. Based on bruises often on her face, she too must fall against treacherous rocks. I will pray her clumsiness has ended and happiness comes her way."

Harey danced around Patrick, avoiding the blurred form of Jonathon seeking to grab ahold of him. "Is Gareth awake and hungry?"

"Yes," Jonathon said. "He was asking for—"

"Me?" Harey dodged again. "I shall unload Bradyn in the garden. First light, I will bring his body to the village. Fare thee well."

Maura sighed. The dark shape racing away, the horse galloping past them to trot alongside, would be Harey.

"Patrick, put me down."

He placed her on her feet and slung his arm around her. "You wish to run as well?"

She sighed. "I wish I had watched the sunset from Gareth's window. How did Harey know to find me?"

Jonathon stepped closer, taking her other side. "He works too hard. He does stop his labors every two or three hours. Not to rest, instead he runs to look upon Gareth and you. When James told him you had gone to bathe, and Harey knew Patrick was not...well, like James informed us, there is not a man, woman, or many animals on this good earth that can move like Harey."

"How..." she faltered. She drew a deep breath.

"Why did Bradyn not head home?"

Jonathon grasped her arm. "He was supposed to clear the rubble from inside the cathedral with his brother. I suspect he saw you cross the field and decided he had a thirst. Wait—my mistake. He was dead at the river bank when you came upon him. I have no idea why he did not go home with his brother and do not care."

"Worry no more of this," Cynric said.

"Yes," said the smaller shadow who must be Eadmar. "I did not like the way that man watched Harey, you...and me as if we were defenseless mice and he a cat wanting to play."

"Mice?" Cynric snorted. "More like mighty rats. You, Eadmar, could spread disease with just one bite."

"Arsehole," Eadmar said. "On the morrow, you must teach me how to deal with a man who may be an angry brother."

"A blow to the cock. A kick in the balls. A rock to his head. How many times must I show you?"

Jonathon released Maura and chuckled. "Methinks the lad now likes you teaching him, Cynric. You are both an affront to heathens everywhere."

The men's banter, their low voices washing over her, and it was as if Harey had not just cleaned blood from her face. She felt so dirty, lifting one heavy foot after the other until somehow the back entrance to the abbey was there, looming in front of them.

She tugged loose of Patrick. "I thank you. I shall go to rest...."

A flickering light, a carefully held oil lamp approached. A small bowl filled with animal fat with a long wick at its center shone light on the face of the man holding it.

"The men rest easy? Gareth?" Patrick asked James.

"All men but one. Harey runs about like a hound

after a hare. He wants help in the kitchen."

Maura made to stumble the opposite way, down the hallway for the bedrooms.

"You too, lass." James shoved the oil lamp into Eadmar's hands. "He insists. Patrick, go flatten Gareth before he unties himself from the bed or worse, removes the gag I placed upon him. Jonathon or Cynric, you best help. Gareth is in a foul mood."

"You restrained him?" Maura could not manage to harden the wobble from her tones. "Why?"

"He is to learn patience and to share." James took her elbow and she found herself headed as he wished. "'Tis a strange night, and Harey is the king in need of a queen. We humble servants do as he bids with joy in our hearts. Just come see."

The oil lamp Eadmar carried was not needed the moment they reached the kitchen area. A roaring fire lit the room, the kettles hung over it. In the corner by the large wooden tub, three flickering candles sat.

A low stump pressed up against a small raised platform had been positioned over where she knew the drain to be. Harey stood beside it, his large eyes black in the dim light.

"Maura, kneel in front of me," Harey said. "The rest of you louts, empty the hot water into the tub, refill the kettles to heat more, and find whiskey and food."

Eadmar set the bowl of light on the table while Harey continued, "James—drag her over here and go fetch your harp. Hurry, before some big man comes to take her attention from me."

A moment later, Maura knelt on the hard stump, bent to lean against the raised board with her hair slung over her head above a large bowl. Harey moved his hand holding her in place, warm water splashed down to soak her hair. Wondrous scents filled her nose and bliss filled her heart as his strong fingers kneaded her scalp. He had dipped his hands into a cup of melted soap, plant oils, and what smelled like freshly crushed rose petals and lavender.

She prayed, fervently, it would never end, and then it got even better. A good twenty men began singing, low and soft, as they filled the tub and sat about the long table, sipping whiskey and eating the bread she had made for the morrow.

Beautiful notes, like the twang of celestial arrows with different sounds as they were released from the bow, guided their voices. She had seen James's harp beside his pallet but had not the heart to ask the grieving student to play it. Gareth had told her that James had made it out of fibers from the hemp plant, coated with the wax of bees to form the strings. Strips of yew wood were glued in a triangle, and a column down the middle allowed him to increase or decrease tension of each string.

After Harey had stopped reusing the water in the bowl, he poured a fresh kettle of warm, almost hot, to rinse her hair. She then found herself upright with three men competing to gently dry her hair using clean tunics.

She did not think her heart could get any fuller, but when Harey combed her damp tresses from her face and pointed her toward the tub surrounded by three tall, thick, and priceless candles made not out of stinking animal fat but sweet smelling beeswax, she recognized the man sitting in an upright rocking chair. The strums of the harp stopped, the men quieted, and her lungs locked.

"Come on, lass," Gareth said. "Get in this pretty smelling water before my big arse takes your place."

She felt her face flush. "Ah...I...will leave the tunic on."

"The hell you will," Gareth said.

"We are not leaving," Eadmar said. "Not while there is still whiskey and bread."

"Then let us ease a lady's mind," Jonathon said. "Men, follow my lead."

Harey guided Maura forward while a group hopped to their feet. Numerous tunics fastened with rope to the ceiling partitioned Gareth and the tub from the rest of the room. A loaf of bread thrown into Gareth's lap, fresh cups of water by the edge of the rocker, and she stepped into the candlelight while the singing resumed. Harey untangled his hand from hers. His gaze downcast, he disappeared under and beyond the hastily-hung curtain.

Her soiled garment disappeared into the dark on the floor. Gareth's bright gaze caressed every inch of her battered skin, and she closed her eyes to the glower filling his face at what had to be numerous scrapes on her front side.

She eased into warm water. The blood of the man she had killed dissipated from her chest, soothing oils caressed her bruises, and it was almost as if a heavy bastard had never touched her.

"Gareth?" she whispered.

"Yes?"

"Harey told you?"

"He did. After I swore not to talk of it or question and comfort until the morrow. I now owe him—and you—my life many times over. Maura?"

"Hmmm?"

"Can I fit in there with you?"

"Are your ribs healed?"

"Yes."

"Liar. The answer is no. I would like a bite of that bread, though."

"Come and get it."

"No. Feed me. I shall never move from this bath.

Lavender, roses, and cinnamon? I love it."

"As you wish. You do know, woman, if I but groan a certain lad who moves like the wind will be at my side with his eyes wide open."

"You do know, man, even if he could tear his sights from you I would not object."

Gareth laughed. He pushed to his feet and took a wobbly step to the tub, bread in hand.

Chapter Ten

Ostara AD 617

 G areth brushed non-existent dirt off the white vestment.

The cloak fit snug in the shoulders, but it had needed little mending and all trace of Connor's blood had leeched out in the sun. It pleased Gareth to know how happy the martyred monk would have been to see him looking this fine. Six months, one week, and two days ago, one thousand, one hundred and sixty-five brothers had left thirty-eight to wear their clothes. Gareth's head, ribs, and arm had healed, but his soul didn't have a rat's arse chance of redemption.

Shivers of survivor joy ran up and down his spine whenever he faced students he had been buried alive with. Hatred hardened his stance if he happened to gaze toward the hills a swarm of killers had swooped down. Sorrow blurred his sight, diluting the color of spring's first flowers he placed on burial mounds.

Shelves, benches, tables, and desks replaced, Gareth hefted the axe for months as he helped rebuild the abbey. With each stroke he imagined a different scenario than a passive protest. He was not a good man, but on this blessed day he would put aside visions of vengeance, speak his vows, and promise to be a faithful one.

The nightfall after he arrived at the massacre, Patrick's hair turned grey. Maura still woke in tears, gasping with memory of brutalities no woman should ever witness. Harey had taken forever to loosen his frantic clutch when Gareth's chest rose too slowly.

Thoughts of the man brought a curve to Gareth's lips. Miracles did happen, and he was beyond grateful the last time he had seen him, the sweet purity of soul still lit Harey's eyes.

He smiled to himself as he recollected Harey's loved voice mumbling by his bedside during his convalescence. The lad who feared women throughout his childhood, and then grew rapidly into an adult to learn men's darkest hearts, had bragged of many a daring raid. Harey grinned as he told of staining boiled eggs to please the little ones and infuriate Argo. Yellow, blues, greens, pink—gay and festive colors—the crumbled, stained eggshells were not what the old sod expected to find under his hens.

While he healed, Harey would help him from their bed and cart him to the rocking chair Patrick had crafted. He would doze and watch Maura and Harey hop about in harmony. Harey would carry in the overflowing basket from the gardens and grab from Maura anything of weight. He would fill the kettle with water and mount it over the fire. Maura would toss carrots in the kettle and in Harey's mouth. He would stare at the ripples in Harey's lean shoulders, the curve of Maura's back, their graceful movements. He had swallowed his moan, the desperate need to hide his hands and relieve the pressure.

Three weeks after Harey pulled him from the

tunnel, the night arrived when the tension had been too much. In the quiet of a room with its door still intact, on a pair of smoky mattresses shoved together, Maura lay snuggled against his healing ribs. Harey sprawled stiffly on the other side of him. His hand brushed Gareth's leg, and he failed to control the rigid tent poking up beneath his robe. Harey had rolled from the furs and padded out into the cold without a word.

The next morn, Harey had whispered in Maura's ear, brushed his lips to Gareth's forehead, and not returned from his run. Maura said he missed Bitty and worried the old hare's heart would give out if it hadn't already, thinking he had deserted her. The stubborn fool had made the return trip to Broch's fortress alone, leaving Patrick to follow a few weeks later. At least Harey had taken the warhorse he charmed away from some pagan bastard. The giant animal would not let anyone else near him, otherwise Gareth feared he would have left the beast to help with repairs and suffered the long journey on foot.

Fall had lived up to its name; warm air tumbled down beneath wintery winds. Maura stood by Gareth's side as he worried about his brother, and whined why had Harey not stayed. Despite the harsh cold, he worked himself into a daily sweat. Pushed healing bones past their limit, chopped enough wood to last a lifetime, shaped support beams and framed windows, unable to stanch the constant ache from missing a brown-eyed man.

Finally, word had filtered through. Blessed by Christ, Eostre, and the abusive witch residing in the stark nunnery beyond the highest falls, Broch survived the battle at Chester with naught but a broken leg. He had been laid up for weeks, managing to return to his castle in time to receive the news Gareth had sent. He requested this spring that his brother, friends, and most of all, his beloved Harey, come to the abbey and bear witness to his vows.

Now, on this long-awaited day, the moon waxed full. It would shine tonight upon a hungry world. With passion, spring would dig itself free from frigid winter as the cycle of life continued. The lunar orb had seen many a terrible thing, great loss and tremendous sacrifice, but hope resonated with each thud in Gareth's chest.

Unfortunately, despite his heart beating strong, he could barely function for the worry churning within him. Patrick had arrived three days ago. Surprised, Harey was not with Gareth; he said Harey had ridden off despite the snows four weeks past, shortly after Broch returned and told of Gareth demanding their presence on this day of Ostara. Patrick thought Harey had decided to shelter one last winter with Gareth while he was still free of vows.

As the hour of commitment and bondage closed in, a twist of fortune he should have accepted years past, Gareth could not help his thoughts turning dark.

Had Brochfael the arsehole tormented him by stirring up talk of a blasted and obsolete fertility rite? Did not their lord know how naïve Harey was, and where the bloody hell had he been all winter? Most important, where the bloody hell was he right now?

Damn Broch. Not like a river of blood had not already polluted the earth, enough to please every horned pagan bastard for generations. The spring goddess did not want the lifeblood of a good man, she wanted renewal and commitment, and Gareth would do his best to see her satisfied.

Please, please, please let him be safe. Let me set eyes upon both my loves this blessed day. Gareth tightened his resolve and departed the prayer room.

Brothers. He averted his gaze as he passed the

crossbeams marking where he had been imprisoned. The monks had forced every student they could grab into that dank hole.

Brother. Broch had managed the retreat of Aethelfrith. With all the chieftains united, they had driven back the Saxon hordes. Gareth was proud of his warrior brother, but he did not know how to ever forgive him for his negligence. In hindsight, it would have made a lot more sense trying to placate their bloodthirsty neighbors instead of a randy goddess or dictatorial Rome.

Harey, how I have missed you. Gareth walked faster. In this moment, he would leave brothers rest in peace. With all his soul, he prayed that a man who was not a monk or relative awaited him.

Seated on new benches in front of the rebuilt cross, the crowd had gathered in the cathedral. The day belonged to sacred vows and Gareth's heart soared with happiness, but the night—his cock jerked, humming with hope—belonged to Eostre.

‹‹ ⠪ ››

Harey peeked around a thick, cathedral pillar. The air slammed out of his lungs, and his cock perked, anxious and hungry. His angel dressed in white looked so wonderful. Blond hair plaited in ceremonial braids, Gareth strode to the front and halted beside Brochfael. His back to the cross, he jerked his attention from face to face and his smile faltered.

Guilt twisted though Harey. He had ridden hard and arrived but a few hours ago. Traitor that he was, he had stayed hidden, praying for some peace within his dark heart. Born a bastard, he had turned against the guardian who rescued him as a child. Gareth would always love him, yes, but not like he wanted him to.

Gareth had said no to him and yes to—

Harey yelped as a little hand walloped him in the back, unsuccessfully trying to knock him from the pillar and into the open.

"Maura?" His jaw dropped. "Oh...oh...oh! You look so...delicious." He fought not to moan. His cock begged for salve and her—*I am so bad*—hand.

"Where the bloody hell have you been? We were so afraid something happened. I have missed you!" Maura flung her arms open. "Kiss me."

Kiss her? It was all he could do to stop himself from jumping on top of her. He wanted to press his lips on every inch of her. His knees wobbled and self-loathing twisted his stomach. *Why, why, why am I so evil*? In a church, lusting for the woman the man he loved was about to exchange vows with, who had been a mother, sister, friend to him? For certain, Harey headed for eternal fires when he died and an aching, solitary bed while he lived.

"No hug, even?" Maura beamed at him. "What are you thinking?"

That I wish I was you. "That you are gorgeous. Too pretty to touch." He grabbed her hand and twirled her. Maura's robe fell to her ankles, and a blue rope hugged her waist. Wide ribbons of color flowed, a riotous pattern of pastels. Pinks edged the hem, yellow kissed her thighs and hips, blue caressed her stomach, light green strips outlined her breasts highlighted with splashes of pink. Her dark hair fell loose about her shoulders, including tiny braids with narrow green ivy twisted through them.

He dragged her farther behind the pillar. "I love your dress. So colorful, I want to eat you. Why are you not up front? Gareth is looking for you."

Maura laughed, sweet and low. Her bright eyes shone with joy. "You are so daft. He is not searching for me, you silly man. He knows his bride is here. Come on." She yanked on his arm.

Harey did not budge. "Maura, go to your husband."

She scowled. "I am not married yet and you are coming with me."

He curled his lip. "You cannot move me. Get."

"Maybe she cannot kick your ugly arse, but I can." A large hand came down on Harey's head. He fought the need to fall to his knees and crumpled into the man. Patrick hugged him. "I am glad you are here, finally, so I can kill you. You have had everyone worried to death. Where have you been, laddie?"

Maura cleared her throat. "Sweet Lord, please. Walk with me before someone changes his mind. Like you, Harey, since I was fifteen I have loved a blue-eyed scoundrel. I have waited forever to wed the man up there, praying for his best friend to be by his side. Patrick, do something, will you?"

Patrick grinned. "With pleasure, m'lady." He grasped and flung Harey off his feet, out and clear of the column.

Harey regained his balance and ducked his head. His face sizzled. Facing the Christ and his followers, he suspected he would burst into flames any second.

"Is that who I think it is?"

"Yes!"

"Harey!"

"Where?"

"There! Harey!" Heads turned, men shouted, and the name of a traitor rang out louder than cathedral bells.

Standing beneath the image of a crucified deity, Brochfael's deep voice boomed, "You ruddy bastards, this is a house of God. Quiet."

Heart in his throat, Harey dared to raise his sights to the most beautiful man in all creation, leaping off the platform to run faster than a hare, a horse, and swooping like a peregrine falcon. Gareth threw himself forward, and Harey would have toppled, if not for Patrick's hand at his back.

"Oh Harey—I feared you were not coming." Gareth embraced him, eased loose, hugged him again, and then stepped back. "Praise God, you are all right." He raked his gaze up and down. "How I have longed for this moment. Where, why, what—sweetheart—I wondered and worried, but for naught. You are here. Finally."

He thought his heart would burst. Gareth looked so happy. *Son, brother, friend, I wish I could be more to him.* "I could never miss your marriage. Gareth? I have to tell—"

"Shh. First, a proper greeting." He threw his arm round Harey's neck and fastened his lips over his gaping mouth.

Harey leaned into Gareth's hold, closed his eyes, and the world melted away. He had never been kissed before, not like this. Gareth's lips felt beyond wonderful, salty and firm as they molded into his. When Gareth's tongue danced, brushing inside his mouth, his moan pulled from his toes and every molecule of flesh, bone, liquid within him began to hum.

Way too soon, Gareth eased his lips away and a low growl forced its way through the rushing waves in Harey's ears. "Not now, you heathen fools," Patrick said. "This is Maura's day."

"Who?" Gareth stepped back, straightened his robe, and his grin widened. "Oh yes, right. Maura. Stand by me, Harey. Sod off, Patrick. Let friends and God witness what his presence means to me." Gareth grasped his hand. He thrust their arms into the air. "Eostre's hare, Christ's saint, has blessed us. Hail to our Harey!"

Men that Harey had carried, fed, and tended while their bodies recovered, swam and laughed with, stomped their feet and called to him as Gareth dragged him down the aisle.

"Arse-loving heathens," Brochfael snapped. "You are before God. Behave, or this wedding will become a burial."

"I am not listening to a word, my liege, unless it is you greeting a hero with respect." Gareth snickered and swung their intertwined fingers. "Have you even thanked Harey for my life? His lips are sweet. Kiss him? Make him welcome?"

Harey clutched Gareth as Brochfael turned scarlet.

Brochfael jerked his hand over his shoulder. "How about I hang him beneath that cross? Argo claims five more hens are missing." He fastened grim eyes on Harey. "I may or may not slit your throat to honor the thirsty goddess, but I do expect hundreds of eggs to replace those taken. Where have you been all winter, you sodden little thief?"

Gareth chuckled. "Dear Broch, this sacred moment is not the time for flawed accusations. Are you completely addled? Harey cannot produce eggs. Fertilize them, no question. A handsome cock—"

"Gareth!" Maura closed in to smack his back.

He untangled his fingers from Harey's and faced her. A low whistle sprang from Gareth's lips. "Sweet Jesus, what happened to Brother Sebastian's robe?"

Harey's turn to hit him. "She is the most beautiful bride in all the world, right?"

Gareth's Adam's apple bobbed. "Oh yes. Of course. Very pretty, lass. Did I tell you I love you?"

Maura rolled her eyes. "Say the right words, good man, before every egg within me dries up." Her smile brighter than the sun, she turned and raised her voice.

"About time Gareth wed me, is it not? Our lord should chastise Eostre's hare for bringing smiles to the children later, right? Did I see barrels of whiskey in the garden?"

"Rope them! Bind them! Marry them!" Strong voices rang out as feet stomped.

Brochfael pulled a white cord from his hip, grabbed Gareth's hand, and slapped Maura's fingers into it. He twisted the rope around their wrists and grumbled, "Idiot. Little brathair, say something."

Gareth raised his gaze from their hands and stared at Maura. He opened his mouth, closed it, opened—Harey kicked him.

"By the power of the heavens," Gareth spoke loud and clear, "mayst thou love me. As the sun stays its course, mayst thou follow me. As light to the eyes, bread to the hungry...."

Harey carefully inched backward. *Gareth kissed me!* No matter he would sleep alone from now on, he would never forget that moment, and the love Gareth and Maura had shared with him. His heart full, he smiled as they kissed. He knew exactly how Maura's knees would be feeling right about now. The couple broke apart, and Gareth raised their bound hands. Everyone cheered and Harey angled to run—right into Patrick's broad chest.

"Going somewhere, laddie? Front garden is the place to be. Men drink and bemoan their lot, while virgins dance round the pole. You must do both."

His grin wide, Jonathon approached, Cynric and Eadmar on his heels. "Think he is still a virgin? Those long nights he lay with Gareth and his lass?"

Patrick clubbed the man. "Lift him, you arseholes. No one sneaks off when there is drink to be had."

Jonathon took one side, Cynric the other, and they hoisted Harey to their shoulders. Gareth and Maura, their wrists still tied, rode on Patrick, Rye, Eadmar, and James. The group burst out of the cathedral. Owen and Vina, Cassie, everyone who had traveled far to honor the wedded couple, called out their names. Local villagers and students who had survived greeted Harey with rowdy enthusiasm.

In the center of the front garden, a tall pole had been shoved into the ground. Ropes twisted and curled from the top to the earth, and gathering baskets of spring flowers stood in each of four corners. A long table overflowed with food, but most people clustered by the whiskey barrels. Lute players and minstrels intermingled with jugglers. Six lasses each held a rope, dancing after each other and giggling as they skipped round the pole.

Like working bees to nectar, Jonathon and Cynric did not drop Harey until they had reached the foremost whiskey barrel. Man after man grabbed at him, their cups overflowing. He tried not to, but he spit out the mouthfuls of bitter drink they forced upon him.

"Come on. Gareth stuck his tongue down your throat, you need something. Swallow."

They laughed, slapped his shoulder, and stumbled for the crowd bustling around Gareth and Maura.

Women eyed and latched onto him.

"Dance with me."

"A kiss? No?"

"You only kiss lads? At least hold me closer."

They pouted until he spun about the pole with them for what seemed like hours.

Deep blue eyes constantly tracked him, but the moment Gareth's back was turned, Harey shrugged free from an intoxicated young lady and trod toward the trees. He could not help his yelp as a large hand clamped down on his shoulder, halting him in his tracks.

"A criminal attempting to flee without my leave is not wise." Brochfael growled and sharp whiskey odor slapped Harey in the face. "Listen. My foolish brother adores you, but I have not forgotten to whom he fated you. The bloody goddess has done nothing for me. If I slit your thieving throat? Then Eostre would bless me with an heir? What say you, ill-begotten thief?"

Harey did not know what emotion shook through him the most, until frustration won out. "Certainly, my liege. The blood of a thousand dead monks did not give you a son? I am sure killing me will raise a limp cock. I should hop up to the altar like a good little lamb?"

Brochfael laughed. "No, it would be more fitting if I dragged you. With respect to Gareth, the fall harvest will suffice. This Ostara, I demand your obedience." He flung a heavy arm around Harey's shoulder and pointed him toward a gaggle of women. "See the fat one? You know my wife. I do not care if you, little cocksucker, hippity hop into her sleeping chamber. She likes blue and green. Put flowers in the basket, too. If I go one more spring with her whining why the serfs get sodden eggs and she does not—I swear I really will sacrifice you to the horned goat who blessed me with that nag. Understand?"

Owen and Vina hurried to the rescue. "Yes, your lordship, he hears you." Vina attempted to pull Harey's arm from its socket and flinched at Brochfael. "Leave the best painted eggies for your wife. We shall see to it he does not forget."

Owen grabbed hold of Vina. He smirked, wide eyes filled with exaggerated fear, at Brochfael. "The village louts are tapping into the last whiskey barrel. Maybe you should go hang a few of them?"

Brochfael snorted. He leaned to Harey's ear. "Many good men perished here. Few remained. See that you stay one of them." He whacked him between the shoulder blades and strode off, leaving him with knees buckling and ground looming.

Owen hauled him upward. "Whew. Close one." Owen snickered. "I worried he would suck your lungs out like Gareth did. Come dance with Vina, before another lame lord tries to molest you."

Harey drew back. "Sorry. My head is spinning." He slapped a silly grin on his face. "I am sure more whiskey will help. Catch up with you later." He headed for Gareth, Maura, and the rowdiest group, and then pivoted to bolt in the opposite direction.

Plump and glowing, a solid moon centered the dark sky. Crisp air burned in and out of his chest, fueling the anxiety and depression churning within. He sprinted so fast he almost crashed into the ancient oak cornering the woods and field behind the abbey.

Harey fought his tears as he collapsed to lean elbows resting on the lowest branch. He had made a decision and he would stick to it. The newlywed couple did not want him hanging about. After Arion stuffed his stomach, and he found where Bit had scampered off to, Harey would begin his life as a sort of guardian. Cursed and spat upon for being a traitor, he would become a lone wolf. He sighed. Wolf? Not likely. Prey instead of predator, he would still do his best to hinder those he loved from wielding the sword and being gutted in return.

The breeze shifted, and Arion raised his nose from the crunchy clover. He whinnied and trotted over. Harey stroked his neck. "Time to stop chewing, my friend. We have to get started. Hunt old, fat Bit down. Maybe she ran into a tree, like I almost did, and then got confused. We will leave as soon as I find her, right?"

"Over my dead body."

Arion snorted, reared, and Harey almost jumped

Harey

out of his skin. "Gareth?" he squeaked, peering through thick branches.

"Yes. I would come over and strangle you, but that beast might object."

Harey could not help the jitters of joy exploding, prancing around inside his stomach. "Arion—you know Gareth. Behave." He slapped the horse on the flank, and Arion ambled toward the choice grasses.

"Late for my wedding, you have not stayed one night, and once again, you were not going to bid me farewell?" Gareth strode around the oak. "Where the sodding hell are you off to?"

Harey's lungs locked up. He never expected to see Gareth in the light of the full moon without a crowd around them. Not this night, the man's wrists bound but a few hours ago. Maybe he would never be alone with him again. Too bad his angel looked like he would reach for an avenging sword any moment. Beautiful blue eyes flashed, dark and dangerous.

Words clogged in his throat, fingers twisting at his tunic, his muscles braced to bolt.

"Talk to me, sweetheart." Gareth softened his tone. "Something has happened to Bitty?"

Harey swallowed hard. "I left her to feed and then could not find her. That is why I was late. She should be here with Arion." Maybe he could get away with ignoring the other questions. Gareth's hatred was inevitable, but Harey could not bear facing the actual sight of his disappointment and fury. It would be so much better if he disappeared before he learned the truth.

Gareth raised his finger, his brow furrowed with frustration. "Do not dare run off before you have answered to me. You cannot blame your pet when you should have been here weeks ago. I am sure the old hare's around here somewhere. But bloody hell—where have you been all winter? And where, who are you running to?"

"I...you will get upset. I do not wish to taint a festive occasion. Go back, Gareth. You should not unbind with Maura on this night."

"I have no worries over her, sweetheart." The dark and dangerous light in Gareth's gaze turned into hot and furious. "Speaking of my bride, her dress is one colorful mess. We both know she did not wear that for me. Harey, have you remained true?"

He could not believe he had heard right. Gareth wondered if he had betrayed him? Well, he had, but not by lying with his woman. "I—I love Maura. But I never slept with her when you...I did but, Gareth, do not be crazy. Any bairn will be yours. She loves you."

Gareth's jaw twitched. "If not Maura, then someone else? There must be reason you fear to tell me where you have been."

"I...sought redemption. Sorry. It will be hard for you to understand." *Right. He'll understand with ease. Forgiveness is what shall not happen.*

"Redemption? I am asking about your body, not your bloody soul. Just tell me. Are you fit for a goddess or not?"

"No, I have not fucked Maura or anyone so yes, I remain a damn virgin." Harey stepped back, his shoulders slumped. "Brochfael sent you? He wants his sacrifice?"

Gareth slapped himself in the forehead. "I have told you. Fating you to Eostre seemed the best way to protect you at the time, and thankfully, you have almost grown into a man who no longer fears women or men—except me. Why is that?"

Harey opened his mouth and nothing came out.

Gareth sighed. "Harey, please. You are so naïve, easily manipulated. I cannot abide you becoming estranged and away from my protection. I want you here. In my arms. In my bed."

Knots filled Harey's stomach. He glanced to the sky, and then dropped his sights to his feet. How could he rest beside a married man knowing he would spend every waking moment wanting more? If Gareth would not let him go, maybe it would be better to accept this spring moon should be the last a virgin lusted under. Once he admitted his deceit, Gareth would put blade to his throat with ease.

He straightened. "Gareth, I am ready. We cannot risk further massacre if Eostre can be made happy. You will hold the knife, not your brother?"

Gareth rolled his eyes. "Stop being so damn bloody strange. You clearly did not listen to a word I said." The ball in his throat bobbed. To Harey's bemusement, a soft grin crept over his face. "Thank the devil, you leave me little choice. Given my way, I will forever remove your doubt. If you are not suitable to slaughter, then you will accept your destiny is to walk this earth with me." He held his hand out.

Harey's mind hummed, as his eyes and ears feasted. Hard to concentrate with his senses racing around like a chicken with its head missing. Blond braids glimmered, beautiful in the dappled moonlight. The bracing night air, subtle scent of whiskey wafting from Gareth...would he relish the taste of malted grain if his angel flavored it with his tongue? The kiss in the church had been so wonderful. Worth dying for.

Gareth sighed. His arm still out, he snapped his fingers. "I mean walk with me now, sweetheart, in this moment."

Harey's arm reacted like a bolt of lightning shot into his veins. He grabbed on, wormed his fingers into Gareth's, and hot current became a warm, fuzzy feeling. Too bad they could not stay connected like this forever.

"Talk to me. I know you are upset about something." Gareth guided him toward the woods. "Tell me where you have been and why you fear we—Maura and me—do not want you in our lives, our home, our bed."

Because I would have to rub my cock until it fell off. "I cannot stay. When your brother learns the truth of my stealing, he will have to see me hanged. I am not sorry either. I betrayed him—and you."

"Betrayed me?"

Tellhimtellhimtellhim. "I gave five hens to your enemies."

Gareth halted. He grabbed Harey's shoulders. "What, exactly, are you talking about?"

"I confronted the relatives of pagans who tried to kill you."

"You did what?" Gareth bellowed. He shook Harey so hard he wondered if his teeth would fall out. "You went alone into Aethelfrith's territory?"

"Er...you are hurting me."

Gareth drew in a shuddering breath and released him. "Damn you. How could you risk yourself like that?" Fists clenched, he trembled.

"How could I not?" He shrugged. "But I failed. I left those who returned with bloodied swords breathing. I could not take a single man, let alone harm any of the numerous grieving women."

"Why would you do such a foolish thing?" Gareth snapped.

The reasons seemed obvious. Hope for retribution, enlightenment, and the means to thwart further murderous plans topped the list. Harey fought his shiver. Fury and shock waged on Gareth's face. He had lost so many friends and teachers, and now Harey added to the weight on those shoulders.

He hung his head. "I am sorry. I have brought grief and shame upon you. I do not regret my actions. I only regret I am not man enough to have told you sooner. A coward will still bring good bounty, right?"

"Fuck the gods! Forget sacrifices!" Gareth's chest heaved. "The thought of losing you, sweetheart, I can barely breathe." He reached—then dropped his hand to smack his leg. "What happened? You confronted the devil who ordered the slaughter? Aethelfrith?"

Take my hand again? Please? Sorrow froze the plea in his throat. He opened his mouth—and swallowed hard as a large hand wrapped around his, tugging him to walk.

"Share this latest folly with me. Know that you can never, not ever, be a disappointment." Gareth squeezed his fingers. "Just a bloody idiot I will never let out of my sight again."

Harey drew comfort, the grip on him firm, and words began to tumble out. "I left Bitty's brood in Owen's care. Told them I yearned to see you. Not a direct lie, I imagined looking upon you every waking and dreaming moment, I but avoided saying I did not plan to head for Bangor. I traveled through thick snow. Found a huge Saxon with blood on his sword and leaking from his chest, arms, legs. He accepted water and thought me a friend. Told me the direction I sought, asked me to bring word to his family. I hated him, held him, closed his eyes upon death, and buried him the best I could in frozen ground. A few days later, the smoke from the largest village guided me.

"I entered on foot. Grabbed a lout from behind. Said I would snap his neck if he did not take me to their king or whoever. He laughed. Punched me. Five or six women jumped me, beat me, and then screamed when Bitty made her presence known. After our ears stopped ringing from the squeal of a terrified hare, they backed off like I had grown horns and tail, and gestured me into their fortress where I removed my tunic.

"Bairns stared, giggling at Bitty pressed to my ankle as I stood with my back bared before Aethelfrith's daughter. She took in my scars and listened to me tell of a blue-eyed, blond angel who had rescued me from a witch and showed me the path to becoming a man. Then I described the unfathomable sorrow her blond, blue-eyed father had caused.

"I gave testimony of dark and fair haired monks whose deity preached benevolence. I spoke of the young man whose decaying body my angel clung to when I finally dug him out. Those who had lost fathers, brothers, husbands, lovers learned why I was glad their men were dead."

Gareth untangled their hands and drew them to a halt. He settled his arm around Harey's shoulder, and Harey hardened the wobble from his voice. "Next morn, I began fixing roofs, repairing fences, any chore that needed doing until I left enough wood for the winter beside the huts without a man inside. I returned to your brother's, took what I wanted, and went back.

"I shared the secrets of keeping hens happy with Carina, the daughter of a king defeated not by Brochfael, but some rival pagan named Edwin. Carina told me this Edwin saw her father dead and seized control of not only Deira, but Bernicia as well. I left her with weak threats, claiming Eostre and Christ would smite all, pagan or otherwise, invading the home of my angel with hatred in their hearts. She knows if I learn Brochfael plans retaliation, I will warn her. I said I would bring her ink that I planned to steal from you."

Gareth snatched his arm back. He crossed his arms over his chest. "Parchment, too, so this...woman," he spat the word, "can communicate with you?"

"No. Ink makes a pretty dye." Harey tried to swallow it, but his sob slipped out. "I came to care for our enemies, the little children, and I thought to show them my favorite color. The shade of your eyes." He fought the loss in his stomach, his heart dead as those in countless graves, and slowly raised his chin. "Please. Go celebrate your wedded night. Sacrifice aside, I will always come visit. I promise."

Gareth scowled. "Right. You lied to me and to Eostre. Run off, little hare. Return to dancing and mating under the moon with your pagan, that Carina."

What? Anger seized him by the throat. "I did not fuck her either. I told you. I must be the oldest virgin in the world. Gareth, I cannot stay with you and Maura. Do you not understand?"

"Not in the slightest."

How dense could Gareth be? "You have made a home at this cursed abbey," Harey said. "Your eyes match Carina's. You could be brother and sister. And until your brother lives in peace with her, the murdering Saxons, I will play the simpleton. Bribe them with eggs. Make sure they are not restless and looking for a thousand more men to gut. They seemed good people, Gareth, do you not believe me?"

"I do not know what to believe, and I will have the truth. Stay as you are. Do not move until I say." Gareth stomped away. Twenty paces into the field he halted and faced Harey. He flung his arms out and yelled, "Greet me properly. Prove you have been true to me."

Moonlight sparkled around the figure poised like a crucified god.

"Come on, you sodden little virgin. Are you a man? Finally?"

The blood in Harey's veins sizzled and roared.

He ran, he leaped—he took Gareth down.

Chapter Eleven

I am no angel. Gareth's shoulders slammed into the ground. A heavy body covered him, and the adrenalin jolting through him made him feel like a powerful animal. *But I am in heaven.* He tugged his arms free, wrapped them around Harey, and grasped the back of his head. *And I do not care if adulterous sodomites go to hell.* He jerked him upward and took his lips.

No time for tender exploration. He had to show him who he belonged to, and it was not some bloodthirsty deity, or the daughter of a mass murderer. What if Aethelfrith, the devil who had ordered one thousand, one hundred and sixty-five men killed so they could not pray against him, had still lived? His friend would have walked into his knife with a smile, a pet hare, and promises of painted eggs.

I will not let this man leave me again. Never. Not ever. He's mine. Gareth fought back his moan and deepened his kiss. The lad tasted so good, fresh and sweet like Maura, but firm and bony where she was all curvy softness. He intensified the pressure, relishing the feel of the lips he had desired for so long, and Harey yielded. Gareth rammed his tongue in, danced around, and then back out to repeat. He had never held a body to mirror his own like this, captive over him, and the sheer joy of not being gentle saturated him.

His beloved lad whose long legs he had dreamed of running his fingers along, firm thigh muscles, the tight curve of his backside, and now actually did so. The experience heightened every raging emotion within him. Aggression filled him, head to toe, centered on his groin. His cock felt thick and longer than it had ever been before, molded against his abdomen, a twin to match the swell of Harey's.

Harey squirmed, tried to arch back, but he held him fast. He yanked the lad's hips upward, their cocks met and kissed, fighting to melt fabric, and Gareth could not halt his groan. One last clash of tongues, he pulled free and gasped.

"Gareth...." Harey moaned. He jabbed his elbow into Gareth's side and wiggled their cocks apart. "Please. You do not have to do this. You are married, remember?"

"Yes, I am not daft. Just in heat." He gulped in another deep breath. "Maybe she...my bride would...er...like to watch."

Harey dropped his hand to the ground and lifted himself off Gareth. He leaned over him. "Watch?"

Gareth choked on lust and rolled. He flipped Harey beneath him. "Maura loves you, too. She knows...well, she thinks you would rather be with a man than a woman. She would give her blessing if I were that man." His cock ached, balls threatened to crack apart, but his heart would be the first organ to detonate if Harey did not lose the blank look and respond to his fingers stroking down his chest. *Please? What do you want?* The sky moved, Gareth grunted, and he found himself under Harey.

"First you say no, then you get married and say yes?" Harey licked his lips, confusion etched on his face. "This does not seem right."

Thankfully, the slope of the ground worked with Gareth. A sharp heave with his elbow and his turn to be on top. "Sorry. I had to wait for you to become strong enough to deny me or not, and then months for you to come back from the most dangerous and stupidest thing you have ever done. Sweetheart, I am not an angel but an arse in love with two people."

"Liar! You. Are. My. Angel." With each word, Harey shoved, pushed, and managed to force Gareth beneath him. He collapsed over Gareth, and he lost all will to move. The feel of Harey blanketing him was wonderful.

Gareth swallowed hard and gazed up into wounded brown eyes. "I am not a good man. Maybe you care for me because I did nothing years ago while Argo shot you, stood by while Broch hit you, and then claimed you for sacrifice so no one would dare to fuck you— until you were ready for me."

Gareth did not tense to warn him. He flipped him fast and hard, and made sure his hips ground into Harey's as he took top again. *Damn. Fun, rolling across a field with my cock on fire.* If he did this with Maura, she would be flatter than an oak leaf by now. He smiled down at the man beneath him. "What if you would be happier with a woman of your own? Bairns with your soft, sweet eyes? At least a dozen lasses danced round that pole with you. I watched and envied each groping one of them."

Muscles rippled, Harey tightened beneath Gareth. "Get off."

His cock screamed no, his heart splintered, but he eased himself backward to his feet. Harey scrambled to stand. He whistled, low and urgent, and Gareth listened to hooves thud behind him.

"I cannot let you leave my protection," Gareth snapped. "I will not touch you again, if that is your decision...Harey? Please."

Harey caught hold of the warhorse nuzzling him and leaped with the grace of a mountain lion onto the creature. "You want me to find a woman? Let us go then."

"Oh thank Christ." Gareth gasped. "I would have you safe in a lass's bed, rather than run off into this evil world on a mission to hide eggs in the homes of murdering bastards." The horse shied. "What must I do to keep you with me?" Gareth could not even get his leg partially up. "Sweetheart...can you help me?"

"Arion, be still." Harey slapped the horse's neck and grasped Gareth. He hauled him until he could swing his leg over. "You do not have to fuck me," Harey mumbled, "so I would believe you care. I know that." He clicked his tongue and the horse lurched forward. "The only reason I understand what love is, is because of you."

Gareth flung his arm around him. "Love, hell yes, but I have yet to clarify lust." He struggled to raise his voice over the rush and clump of the biggest beast he had ever ridden. "You are the wondrous angel, not me. A saint, most worthy soul I know. In the tunnel, it was not any goddess or Christ I prayed to. I had no doubt if anyone came to resurrect me from a grave, it would be you."

His beloved Harey must understand his intentions were nothing other than a relentless, wanton need. A desperate hope indulging in sins of the flesh would bind two men tighter than a wedded white cord. He snuck closer.

"The first time I laid hands and sights on you," Gareth said, lips so close to kissing Harey's ear. "I knew you were blessed with a pure heart. Before gods, abusive woman, and brother, I marked you for my own. Now, this night, please—I must lay claim."

The rise and fall of the horse's flank, hoofs pounding up and down, Gareth's cock grew hungrier with every grind against it. Harey guided the beast around the abbey the long way. Dare he hope he did not want this ride, the presence of a cock determined to have another, to end too soon?

I cannot resist. He bent, licked, and nibbled along the curve of Harey's neck, his lips rejoicing in the erratic pulse beating against his mouth.

Harey moaned. "Do not."

"Do." But Gareth eased back and drew a deep gulp of cooling air. "Sweet. You taste better than I imagined as I lay in darkness, not sure if I was alive or dead and in hell. My head throbbed like I had been axed in the skull. Thirst overwhelmed me. If I could have moved to gather my piss, I would have drunk it. I floated in my happy place while I waited for you. That meadow. Hares dancing. The full moon shining like it does now. Your hand in mine and in my dreams, I told you yes."

Harey stiffened. "In my dreams, you had not taken vows. Maura—she deserves better. How can I abuse her kindness by stealing you from her on your first wedded night?"

Because I must and will have you both. Gareth smiled. He would seduce this man if it was the last thing he did. He pressed in, knowing Harey could feel the swell of his purring cock as it rubbed the tunic, the crease of his arse. He nipped at the back of his ear, worked against him, and murmured, "Take a woman or take me, but know what Maura and I want, more than anything, is for you to stay with us. Always."

A clenched sob fell from Harey's lips and he went in for the kill. He eased his hand beneath the tunic, and ran his fingers along Harey's thigh. "Try to leave and I will...bloody hell, I could go with you." He reached the taut muscle of inner thigh and headed for the curve of what promised to be tightened balls. "You could raise blasted hens here, with me watching over you. Then I will help you distribute them, Patrick and his axe along for sport." Gareth brushed Harey's cock through the thin pants. *Rigid, long, thick....*

Harey snapped, "Stop that."

"No." He forced his hand lighter than a feather, caressing his thumb inch after inch after inch, curling over the crest. "Why do you have to give out the spring baskets?" he rasped. "Cannot parents do it?"

"Ah...yes. Gareth...please. I fall, and you are coming with me."

Coming with? As in two cocks gushing seed together? Christ, yes. Harey's moan echoed his, and he slid his hands to the shelter of thick leg muscles, before he attempted to fuck his first man while on top of a trotting warhorse. A selfish bastard, he was not being fair. If only his resolve could harden as firm as his cock. The ride would end very soon. Harey would knock the devil behind him off, leaving him sprawling on the ground. He would gather up whichever lass had caught his eye, the pair would ride off into the sunset, and he would be left holding to a thwarted cock and a lost dream.

The ruckus of celebrating drunks accosted his ears, and Gareth dragged his gaze from the ripples in Harey's backside. They cantered into the front garden. All attention fastened on the giant steed descending upon them.

"Ah, should you not slow...Harey!"

Harey leaned to the left, and the stallion swung around Broch and Argo like the animal was an extension of his body. They plowed past a drunken Patrick, galloped beyond the wondrous grin on Jonathon's face and Cynric's jaw on the ground.

An elbow aiming for his chest, Gareth jerked

backward, Harey dipped down, and the next thing he knew, Harey snagged up the most beautiful woman, in the most festive dress. Gareth grabbed hold of arms while Harey straightened and urged the horse onward.

"Ohh," Maura yelped. "Harey, Gareth, do not drop me!"

"Harey, you pagan bastard. Slow down!" Gareth shifted onto the horse's rump and swung his bride in front of him. "Maura, hang on to him."

Faces passed in a blur. The stallion reared up, jumped over the trellis, came down hard, and continued racing around the cathedral.

Maura clung to Harey's back, and Gareth smashed her into him so he could yell in Harey's ear. "Where are we going?"

Maura squirmed and he thought his frantic cock would wrap itself around his leg and strangle him. He needed to be inside one of his loves soon, or seed would shoot out every orifice to please the air and his robe, instead of a sweet, tight passageway.

"Left, Harey. Down by the creek. Take us home." Maura giggled. "Cannot this horse go faster?"

The little she-devil could feel Gareth's desperation. His cock hammered against her, her breasts molded into Harey, the pounding rhythm between their legs, it all felt so right. Gareth had to somehow maintain this bond.

Three.

They belonged together.

Harey guided the horse toward the woods, and they cleared the field.

Everyone had helped build the little wood and thatched straw castle sitting between thick trees, bordered by the gurgling creek and a fenced enclosure for the dozen hens and one cock. Argo had given the fowl Harey had not managed to steal yet to Gareth and

Maura. It was the old sod's way of apologizing to the lad he had marked with an arrow years ago.

"Whoa—it looks wonderful here, does it not, Arion?" Harey clucked the horse into a rough halt. He twisted to glance at Gareth and Maura. "This—your home is lovely. How did Bit know you were here?"

"Whaaat? This is your home, too. Harey? You listening to me?" Gareth followed Maura's gaze. The hare shot from the bramble to scamper toward giant hooves. Her hind legs tensed and Bitty sprang while Maura went tumbling, Gareth right after her.

"Harey!" Maura gasped.

"Bastard," Gareth grumbled as he gathered his wife from the ground. Harey had pushed them off so he could easily catch his pet. Gareth brushed dirt from his bride and slung his arm around her. They stared at Harey clutching the hare, stroking her and mumbling.

"Oh yes, I worried about you, my true friend. You never yell at me. Never leave me for some god who almost gets you killed. Marry a woman and then kiss...."

Harey slumped. He slowly raised his chin, his thin face twisted with apprehension. "I am sorry, Maura. My fault, not his. I kissed him. Will not happen again. I shall stay with Owen for the rest of this night. I promise I will not go off without telling you."

"Oh no, you are not." Maura shrugged free of Gareth. She stomped forward, the horse raised a hoof, pawing the ground and she froze. "You are staying here. Bitty found us because she knows this is your home. See those hens? Think I want to take care of them? Get down off that beast and stop lying. Tell me exactly what my husband did to you."

Harey flinched and Gareth stood there, his heart pattering worse than a cornered hare. Maura scowled at the sheepish smirk on his face, and her attention spun back to Harey. "That blue-eyed devil kissed you again? Like in the church?"

Harey tossed Bitty down and slid off the horse with his shoulders hunched. Gareth thought his heart would break. He ached to scoop Harey into his arms, but another evil glance from Maura suggested he had best let her take the lead.

She glowered, hands on her hips, until Harey stepped clear of the horse. "Did not that idiot explain anything to you?" she closed the gap between them. "Harey, listen. If I have to share Gareth, then so be it. I do not care what anyone thinks of us, how often...or where you put your mouths in the privacy of our home. I would love for you to kiss me, too, but Gareth surely kisses better than ten thousand men put together, so it matters not to me if you want to be...er...intimate only with him."

Finally, the dazed look lifted from Harey's eyes. He raked his gaze over Maura like he had never seen her before. "He does kiss nice. If I can outrun, I am sure I can out-kiss him as well. You would like me...with you? Really? A kiss like a man does, not a lad to his mum?"

Maura gasped. Her hand flew to her mouth. "You think of me as your mum? God, Harey. This is complicated, is it not?"

"But she has wondered about humping you for ages. More than—"

"Quiet, Gareth," she snapped. "Why not feed the horse? Except...I fear it might bite your head off. Harey has not eaten. Go cook something."

Gareth snorted. If he moved, it would be to fill his own mouth, and he did not want food. He had wondered about a cock between his lips, a specific one to be sure, for an eternity. And in a matter of minutes, he would have his way with the pair in front of him before his own cock shriveled up and fell off from frustration. How dare Harey, a virgin, expect he could outdo Gareth? Kiss better than him?

Harey inched closer to Maura. "I do not remember parents. Gareth and you are the only ones to care for me like that, but I love how he tasted with his tongue in my mouth. I do not think of him as my da."

Gareth swallowed back his cheer as Harey laid his hand on Maura's shoulder, his gesture as intimate as a lover. "Anyway, if I knew any da, I would hate him. I am a man now, am I not? But...." He leaned to whisper in her ear.

Maura eased back and her giggle, young and carefree, filled Gareth's heart. She beamed at Harey. "Oh no, that is not at all silly. I could show you. You are thinking about it too much. He is easy. Your hands alone will make him grunt with joy. Trust me, I know."

"Bloody Christ." Gareth snarled. "I am standing right here. You are talking about me, right? Harey, what is wrong? Talk to me, too. You used to share everything with me. Are you wondering how to go about this?"

"Yes...this...does not seem real." Harey wilted, all confidence gone. His eyes glassy, his face flushed. If not for Maura's hand jumping to clasp his arm, Gareth suspected he would have bolted.

Gareth swallowed hard. "Reality does not matter, as long as the dream pleases you. You are not alone in feeling nervous. I need to learn, as well. Never kissed a woman other than Maura and a man other than you— well, willingly that is. My fist ended it fast. I do not know positions, what you would like, any of that. But I will have you both. Now. Sooner than now. Please. Should we pair off or try something all together? Maura?"

She rolled her eyes. "Yes. I am the expert. Harey, give me a kiss. If it feels right, you could carry me into our home while Gareth fetches, you know, something to ease his way or your way, if it comes to that. If my kiss feels immoral or bad, then, well...." She tugged Harey's arm and he bent to her whisper.

Harey laughed. He straightened, tossed a delicious smile at Gareth, and shot his arm beneath Maura's legs, sweeping her into his arms. "Thank you. I would like that, very much."

"What, what would you like?" Gareth had been hard and aching for what seemed like years, but the sight of Harey's mouth fastening onto Maura's—he fought his hands reaching for his cock, while his heart jumped so fast against his ribs he thought he would drop dead. If something was unstable inside him, a lacking only two could fill, he was about to join with a man and a woman as close and completely as humans could. *I will storm heaven's gate.*

His cock roared, his muscles tightened, and lightning filled his veins. He watched the pair still kissing as Harey strode off, effortlessly carting Gareth's bride.

My lad has become strong, virile, and able to knock me on my arse. He does not like me in his arse, he will stop me. Gareth did not walk, he ran for the pouch with salve in it he had left in the stable.

Ointment in hand, he burst through the door and shivered with anticipation.

Harey had laid Maura on the large bed. His knees on either side of her hips, he loomed above her while she tried to wiggle out of her dress, and Harey stopped her. Gareth tugged his cloak and tunic off, tossed them, and hurried to yank his feet out of his pants.

"Please. The dress is so beautiful. Leave it on. You are so beautiful. Are you sure this is right? I can...Gareth?" Harey's eyes went wide. He stared at Gareth's cock, jutting out hard and dripping.

Gareth smiled and reached for him. He grabbed him around the hips and lifted him off the bed. Once he had him on his feet, he grasped Harey's tunic and began to pull it over his head. "What did she say to you, sweetheart? Maura, I do not give a damn what he wants, remove that dress before I rip it off you."

Gareth flung Harey's tunic aside and gazed at the dark wisps of hair running down his chest. He reached, trailing his fingers down, halting his hand to lay flat above the tie to Harey's pants. He swallowed the pooling moisture in his mouth at the sight of the large bulge, and looked to Maura. "Do tell, my wife, who kisses better, me or him?"

Maura laughed. "Ahh, that is a difficult question to answer. You must keep competing. And why can I not play as well? Do tell, my husband, who kisses better, me or him?" She slowly unfastened the strips of bright ribbon binding her breasts in place. "Hmm. Man to man. Man to me. Another man to me. I am sure it will take a lifetime to decide. Now, Colin, he is a very good kisser."

Harey clamped his jaw closed, jerking his sight from Gareth's hand to Maura. His growl rang louder than Gareth's. "I thought I ran that sod off. He dared to kiss you? You...let him?"

A gorgeous red tinge filled Maura's cheeks. She shook her head, lowering her attention to the ribbons. "No, no, sorry. I do not know why I said that. I am thinking too much. Maybe I should let you men...well, I know you have waited so long for each other."

Oh Lord, my bride is nervous. Worried she is not what our virgin wants. He watched Harey's gaze dart between them. He had best take charge. Elder by three years, much experience, his bloody cock could wait...not long. Ah well, if he burst into the air, he would harden back up soon enough with faces like these to feast upon. The spellbound lad as lovely as the lass.

Harey, eyes wide and round as the spring moon, watched as ribbons fluttered aside. His pupils darkened, dilated, and heated as he took in bared breasts. Gareth swallowed hard and chuckled as Harey did the same. "Maura, sweetheart, look at our lad."

Maura glanced and blushed prettily to match Harey. Her movements as dainty as a butterfly, she eased her dress off. "Oh. I would let our lad do whatever he wanted, but taking this long for my men to undress makes me wonder if I should step aside."

"Move from that bed, you shan't get far," Gareth said. "And make sense, woman. I cannot get any more naked. Harey, up with...well, I see a certain part of you is as up as I am. Get those pants off. You all right, sweetheart?"

"No. I am sorry. I fear I shall wake up...or mess up." Harey stumbled as he pulled at his pants. "She...she said I could learn on her first. Then I would last longer, please you better. Then maybe I can make you happy. Right, Gareth? I do not want to muck this."

Gareth fell to his knee. He grabbed hold and ran his fingers down Harey's leg, slow and sensual, enjoying the feel of tense muscle. "There is naught you can do to make me happier than I am right now. Relax. Let me...let us show you."

He lifted Harey free of the pants, stood and kicked them aside. Poised on the bed, Maura leaned on her elbow taking in every detail. She ran her tongue over her lips and Gareth's balls became even more constricted, so much so he feared the pebble-hard flesh would soon splinter. Another drop escaped, sliding from the slit in his raging cock.

Harey's cock grew out from a curly dark nest, thick and long, juices dripping to match Gareth's, and he knew if he did not soon give in to his need, just a little taste, his head would explode. A strangled gasp drew his attention higher. Harey stared at him.

"Sweetheart?"

"This is real? I am to be yours and I can have Maura, as well?"

"Yes. For right and wrong, sickness and health, dreaming and awake. One thing first." He grasped above Harey's wrist. "Take hold of my arm...no, dear lad, the arm of the hand holding your arm."

Before Gareth even held his other hand out to Maura, she had hopped from the bed and taken hold of his fingers. Lovely breasts swaying, she dipped to grab Harey's hand.

Finally, Harey's fingers stopped trembling on Gareth's arm, his grip as firm as his own, and Gareth held to his gaze as he said, "By the power of the heavens, mayst thou love us. As the sun stays its course, mayst thou follow me, your protector. As light to the eyes, bread to the hungry, eggs to heathen bastards, do you swear to love and obey until death do us part?"

His lips quivering, Harey whispered, "yes."

"Yes! Maura, he said yes! What say you?"

"Oh yes." She dropped their hands and retreated for the bed. "Seal the oath."

Their hands still clasped on each other's arm, Gareth pulled him inward. Hard and rough, he kissed him and Harey returned the lust. Fast and hungry tongues did not explore but plundered. Arms fell to wrap around backs, fingers splayed and dipping into the curve of the arse. Cocks banged, brushing and grinding happily into each other until Harey groaned, pulling his lips free to pant. "Gareth, I...what should I do?"

"Fuck." He walked Harey backward. "Take Maura.

She is wonderful. You will think you are in heaven." He lifted him and seated him on the edge of the bed. "It will be fine, I promise. You can love our lass any which way she and you please. But first, a selfish man, I will ready you."

Maura started to scramble aside, and Gareth halted her with a grasp of her leg. He tugged her forward, and pushed Harey so his shoulders pillowed against her chest.

The dress lay folded neatly in the bed's corner and Gareth smiled. "Let us see if we can add some white to a colorful mess of a wedding gown, shall we?"

"White?" Harey squeaked. He peeked at Maura wrapping her arms around him.

"Yes," Gareth said. "We will make it sticky and salty, too. On second thought, I may not let a drop splatter onto it."

"Gareth?" Harey groaned.

Do it. Now. Gareth's knees hit the floor. He eased one hand on Harey's thigh, and wrapped his other around the base of a cock for the first time other than his own, and tried to stop himself from humping straw as he lowered his mouth for the pulsating treat in front of him.

Strange. Wonderful. In and out. Up and down. The feel of the thick cock between his lips, down into his throat, was exciting, yes, but nothing like the shivers of pleasure running along Gareth's spine as he listened to the gasps, grunts, gulps coming from Harey. He licked along a pulsating vein, and sucked over the crest. When he pushed his tongue into the thin, oozing slit, Harey arched his hips, and Gareth pulled his mouth free. He smacked his palm on Harey's stomach, pressing him down. He licked the sap off his lips, swallowed and raised heavy-lidded eyes.

Harey fisted the gown, his other hand fluttering for

Gareth. Maura, her smile wide, grabbed his arm. "Shh, love. Let me help." Maura twisted out from under Harey and moved in front of Gareth to swing her leg over Harey's chest. Gareth caressed Harey's balls, yanking gently to stall him from erupting, and lowered his eager mouth.

Harey sobbed and writhed as Gareth drew his cock into his throat harder, deeper before pulling out to slowly lick. He trailed his tongue over the sensitive tip, and Harey's gasping became desperate. Gareth released him, smiling at the ecstatic daze in his expression, and clasped Maura's hips. He positioned her over Harey.

Maura lowered her head for Harey's kiss, he wrapped his arms around her, and Gareth let go of the pair. He grabbed hold of his cock, jerking his hand to slam against his balls, while he again licked the flavor of a man's juice from his lips.

Harey groaned, eyes rolling as he broke loose of Maura's kiss to collapse backward. She raised her lovely body and mounted him. Joy thrilled through Gareth as he watched her ease herself down Harey's cock. He closed in to press into her back, his cock grinding between her arse cheeks. He leaned, took Harey's face between both hands, and kissed him. The thought of Harey tasting the happiness in Gareth's mouth, whiskey sweetened by his own juice, it felt like angels sang within his heart.

Time to take this lad into heaven. He bent his legs, used his chest, and urged the woman smashed between them into a hard ride up and down Harey's cock. He jabbed his tongue in and out of Harey's mouth in harmony with Harey's thrusts into Maura.

As Harey sobbed his orgasm between Gareth's lips, emptied his seed into Maura, she cried her release into Harey's shoulder and clenched herself around him—

Gareth knew he had found the balance he had yearned for all his life.

ɶ

Maura sprawled over Harey and spiraled down from the clouds. He still throbbed, partially hard within her. Those long beautiful lashes fluttered, he opened his eyes—and panic spilled.

"What is wrong?" She slid off him and rolled to the side.

"Sweetheart?" Gareth knelt on Harey's other side.

Harey blinked hard and stared at Gareth. "I-I did not pull out. I am sorry. I messed up."

Maura brushed her fingers along Harey's arm. "Would you stop being daft? Messed up? Never. You were wonderful." Maura allowed her affection to color her face with joy. "If you have given me a bairn, I shall be the happiest mum in the world. A baby for the three of us to love? I would like that. Very much."

Harey twisted to stare at her. "Even if I am the da?"

Gareth chuckled. "It matters naught whose seed hits the egg. As long as you do not ever leave your— our—little one, like your da did. And Harey? There is not a chance you shall win the race. I do not care how fast your legs can move, they do not release the seed." He leaned on Harey and smacked a kiss on Maura's lips. "Soon as I get in you, I will beat any lame runners he shot out."

"Yes, you will empty quite soon, I fear." She laughed and eyed Gareth's lovely, yearning cock. He had been so good, waiting and easing Harey's first time. "Oh my. You are dripping those runners right now. And so huge. Almost as big as you, right, Harey?"

Gareth growled. He slammed Maura down and turned to Harey scrambling out of the way. "Ah, thank you, sweetheart. I know you are not running off, but getting behind me, behind her, anywhere you would like to be as long as we are touching."

Maura nodded. "Yes, this is our time with you, Harey. Anything you want."

Delicious brown eyes went wide. He inched closer for her ear. "Can I hold you while he fucks? Then he can...do what men do with me?"

Gareth slid his hand between her legs. His gaze, eyes brighter than the clearest sky, on Harey. "Yes, hold her and feel me inside her, but what if my cock is too thick for you? I know...well," he looked at Maura. "You never seemed as if you wanted me like that. What if I hurt him?"

"Then you stop, silly man." Maura lifted herself, shifted and squirmed until Harey settled behind her. She leaned against his chest, and wiggled into Gareth's hand. Soaked with Harey's seed, she did not think she could get any wetter.

She was wrong. Pure joy gushed from her center as Gareth grabbed Harey's hand, placed it on her left breast, and then leaned to take her other breast into his mouth. Harey's breath hitched, his fingers rolling her hardened nipple as Gareth's tongue rasped over the other.

Gareth raised himself up. "Har, both hands."

Strong fingers cupped her breasts while Gareth eased his cock into her an inch, and then plunged so hard and deep she could not tell where he ended and she began. He rocked his hips, moaning at Harey. "I will not attempt to take you like this first. You must do whatever you want, whenever you want, to my arse, and then tell me what you would fancy. Right?"

"I...don't...."

The ripples, tightness in her stomach warned her she would not last long much longer. She had better take charge of her men. "Gareth, hold on. Do not move until I say, then remember this is our first time, husband, without holding back and withdrawal."

Gareth gasped. "Sweet Christ, I forgot. Oh...." He raised, his cock jerking within her as he pulled back readying to slam down.

"Did I say you could move?" She grinned at the heat filling his face as he froze. Harey's fingers lightened on her breasts, trembling. Pinned beneath Gareth's quivering body, she would twist to glance up at Harey if she could. "After this, Harey, we will rest like we usually do, Gareth in the middle. You shall have his back, and I will watch his face and tell you what fun he is having. That is, if he does not make enough noise for you to figure it out. No reason to rush. I do not expect any of us wish to sleep this night, or many more to come. We have a lifetime to perfect ourselves."

Glassy brown eyes loomed over her shoulder. Harey nodded, and Maura looked to Gareth. Hot blue eyes snapped and crackled with tension. She giggled, clenching her muscles around his cock and Gareth groaned.

"You are killing me, you little witch. Maura, please."

She clamped around him again. "Listen. Harey goes slow, not you. Rush. Hard and harder. Show him we shan't break. Let him see...ohhh...ohhh...sweet...."

He pounded into her, powerful thighs rose upward, driving down again as Harey gulped, hands trembling on her breasts. She glanced up. Harey leaned over her, watching her face as well as the wonderful cock finding its home. She knew then, it was not only the man on top of her making Harey feel safe and loved. He needed her, as well.

Blue eyes and brown, the shades blurred, and all the emptiness, lonely years of Maura's life disappeared. Harey left her breasts, wrapped strong hands on her hips, pushing her to take Gareth so deep she thought he would merge into her.

Gareth brushed her lips with his, groaning and gasping his happiness while Harey and Maura did the same.

ભ

In the year of our Lord, AD 618

Sweat trickled down Harey's face and splattered off his chin. He leaped, twisted, and maintained his speed. Bliss filled him, head to toe. They had shared over a wonderful year together since Gareth and Maura bound their wrists.

Last fall, Gareth had ridden with Harey into three Saxon villages. He had hovered with his hand on his knife, even when bairns rushed out screaming with joy, pulling at Harey's tunic to find Bitty.

He had insisted the escort of fifty men with big heavy swords leave the woods to join them when they approached the largest settlement. No words for Carina, but he nodded when Cynric said he, James, and Eadmar would stay to teach letters, the ways of a peaceful God, and most important, how to care for the hens and make the prettiest of dyes.

This past spring, Gareth did not glower at smiling parents holding out little baskets for Harey to fill. His gaze filled with peace, he had told everyone to spread the word across the isle of Briton that Harey had responsibilities, and there would be no more fall, summer or winter visits. Only when the moon was full and the flowers pushed up from thawing ground would Harey run carelessly into their villages. While the spirits of one thousand, one hundred and sixty-five men watched, none would dare raise their hand to Eostre's chosen.

Harey still did not understand the obsession with deities. The luckiest bastard on this earth, no deity had ever spoken to him, let alone yet taken his life blood or his heart. He had been chosen by a man and a woman, and his flesh, his mind, his soul belonged to them.

This morn, Harey had felt the bairn drop. Maura would birth their child soon, and Gareth would have to cook for a month. Harey knew he would win the bet. He had said a lass with huge blue eyes. Gareth had said no, a lad with delicious brown eyes. Maura claimed the bairn could have one blue, one brown, and as long as there were two eyeballs, why would they care the shade? Then she had said both her men were daft, always forgetting the strongest carried sway, meaning the eye color would be as green as her own.

A basket with herbs to ease Maura's labor on his arm, Harey hopped over a fallen branch and curved for home. He loved to run fast with old fat Bit scampering on his heels, but he no longer dashed and darted in a line as straight as the forest would allow.

Round like the sun, oval like the egg, his protective orbit had grown circular. His star, the yolk in the middle, would be the babe he would hold any hour now—his loves beside him.

~ABOUT THE AUTHOR~

Sci-fi, paranormal, suspense, indefinable, Arlene Webb is an author who adds sweet and spicy layers of romance. She was born in upstate New York, land of cows, snow, drizzle and sometimes a ray of sun. Second oldest with four siblings, she spent childhood reading everything she could get her hands on. Adolescence found her questioning the validity of everything she read, along with acquiring the usual scars of high school.

Early twenties, she headed for the Pacific. A stop off to visit a friend turned into years in Tucson, Arizona. Arlene worked as a waitress, bartender, greenhouse worker, greyhound trainer, while swapping a pysch major for one in plant sciences at the University of Arizona. Fired for skipping employee meetings at restaurants, employee gambling at the dogtrack, refusing to use live rabbits as bait, it fell to planting cacti and bartending to pay her way through college.

Arlene's late twenties found her running family owned greenhouses and florist shops in New York. When the reality of retail life became too mundane to handle, she began an obsessive love of creating more interesting worlds.

Visit Arlene online at:
www.arlenewebb.com

www.ingramcontent.com/pod-product-compliance
Lightning Source LLC
Chambersburg PA
CBHW071719140626
46557CB00012B/968